THE MESSIAH MATRIX

By

Michael E. Morgan

For information write to:
DawnTrader Books, LLC, P.O. Box D7-413
34522 North Scottsdale Rd, Scottsdale, Arizona 8266
Or call: {914) 433- 9363

If you are unable to order this book from your
Local bookseller, or Amazon.com, you may order
directly from the publisher
Quantity discounts for organizations are available.

Edited by Sal Glynn

Cover design by Michael Morgan

ISBN 9 780990 313304 (paper)
10 9 8 7 6 5 4 3 2 1

DawnTrader Books, LLC

DawnTrader Books, LLC

Dawn Trader, Books LLC, is an independent publishing company. To make the world a better place, it must begin on the inside at the core level, where the heart and mind meet, to rekindle that childlike wonder. Where the magic of fantasy and ideas live.

Man needs the imagination where greater possibilities lay hidden inside the sleeping consciousness, which waits to be activated by inspiration. Dawn Trader Books, LLC, seeks to inspire greater joy for life with its stories of inspiration, adventure and spiritual wisdom.

Dawn Trader Books, LLC promise, is make entertaining stories for the reader. Its stories engage the imagination while revealing truths behind many legends, myths and mysteries. Visions of possible futures, curious pasts, and alternate realities invite the reader to awaken the inner potential, and thus begins the evolution of human consciousness and greater wisdom. Adventure and wisdom are sampled within these stories to enhance the quality of life.

Christianity is a religion based on a document called the New Testament. Four books make up the essence of the doctrine—Mathew, Mark, Luke and John. These books make up the official canon on the true life of Jeshua of Nazareth, also known as Jeshua, the Son of God, and Messiah. The accounts in the New Testament depict Jeshua's birth, teachings, and relationship with the twelve disciples, until his death and resurrection, from four points of view. The Greek Orthodox Church disagrees with Roman Catholicism and acknowledges him only as a man and great prophet.

Jeshua threatened the sovereignty of Roman rule and the divine authority of the Jewish Sanhedrin. He performed miraculous feats such as raising the dead, becalming a storm on the Sea of Galilee, and many healings of sick people, casting out demons, turning water into wine, feeding multitudes with only five barley loaves and two fish. At the end of his three-year ministry, he was betrayed by one of his own disciples and brought before the Roman Procurator Pontius Pilate to be judged. Charged and found guilty of sedition, they sentenced him to be crucified.

From 3 BCE to 150 CE, many stories were told about the prophet by people who had contact with him during his life, beyond those of the disciples that spread his word. But hundreds of followers never spoke out, hiding from the Romans. Meetings were dangerous and considered seditious by Rome. The Christians met only in small hovels through Judea, to discuss and debate his teachings among each other. They had little or no contact with other followers, and the movement remained fractured and non-cohesive.

Later, the conqueror and ruler of the known world, Constantine, joined the Christian faith. Disgruntled by its disorganization, he wanted the doctrine to be adopted throughout his realm. In the fourth century CE, he called together a group of scholars and theologians to be known as the First Council of Nicaea.

Constantine regarded the gospels as heretical, except for the four chosen— Mathew, Mark, Luke and John. The council knew even these accounts were dissimilar, and Constantine ordered his scribes to alter the gospels, smoothing over the differences. This cogent and consistent viewpoint between the four represented the official cannon that represented the faith.

The situation stood for centuries until 1945, when a shepherd in the Qumran region of Israel known as Nag Hammadi, dug up urns buried in the earth. At first, afraid they might contain djinn or evil spirits, he did not touch them for days. Then overtaken by curiosity, he broke the urns open. He discovered several scrolls wrapped in leather and written on parchment inside.

These became known as the Nag Hammadi lost

scrolls of the Essenes in Qumran, or the Dead Sea Scrolls.

The discovery rocked the religious and archeological world, and their content became very controversial. They held heretical accounts of Jeshua, hidden from the assaults of Constantine. He was relentless in his search and destruction of the other records regarding the life of Jeshua.

The scrolls left Israel soon after their discovery. From there, they disappeared. Some emerged in various locations years later.

After translating the documents, the contents were very controversial to accepted scripture. Even today, only certain scholars accept the scrolls as valid historical documents. Not all agree. Today the scrolls are considered historical artifacts with little or no acceptance.

The story of Jeshua's life and death has come under scrutiny by modern scientific scholars seeking to verify through historical documents and archeological findings what believers know to be true. It was written that after crucifixion and burial, he arose on the third day and ascended into heaven.

Believers pronounced this as proof of his true nature and divinity, but details of the events in actual history are clouded in mystery. Evidence of carbon dating shows the gospel accounts of his existence only as early as 150 to 200 years after his death and resurrection. This suggests there was no eyewitness at the time of his death beyond those reported in scripture. The Holy Scriptures were transmitted by God, recorded by inspired writers and must be true, which the faithful keep close to their hearts.

According to Hebrew accounts, the lost Ark of the Covenant is not only the chest that contains the broken tablets of the Ten Commandments, but an instrument to speak to God. This meant that the Ark possessed supernatural power, and original biblical accounts spoke of the Hebrews using it as a weapon to decimate their enemies.

Scientists may believe but demand proof of miraculous events and question everything. This reaction is normal for people who place their faith and trust in what they see before them. Scrutiny continues with other biblical accounts, such as the destruction of Sodom and Gomorrah. In fact, an investigation regarding the exact location of those two cities and their fate is currently underway.

In fairness, for many years the archeological establishment regarded the city of Troy described by the Greek poet Homer in The Iliad and The Odyssey was mythological until the city was uncovered.

With this in mind, scientists are hopeful. The investigation of another artifact, the Shroud of Turin, scrupulously examined by carbon dating, disappointed believers and non-believers when a piece of the shroud that allegedly wrapped his body while in the tomb, failed to provide concrete proof of his existence. The 1988 dating suggested it was from the fourteenth century, falling well short of the first century date desired, but believers did not give up.

Evidence of a bad sample declared the 1988 dating invalid; the piece of cloth used was not from the original. Because further access was not allowed, speculation gave rise to hope that another test would concur with the first century proposition. You can imagine the sigh of relief.

Further examination revealed the threads they were given were actually newer threads woven into the edge of the older cloth after a fire in 1532 almost destroyed the shroud. A papal church edict declared the piece the only sample of the shroud available for examination by scientific means. Pockets of resistance refuse to accept this, and believers continue to maintain new evidence will redefined the situation and vindicate their efforts. The controversy continues.

The Messiah Matrix begins where the Shroud of Turin leaves off, suspended in time and cloaked in mystery. What if the shroud is real, and archeological findings like more scrolls of Nag Hammadi are translated to reveal evidence of Jeshua's existence and teachings that might put the believers and non-believers into the same corner?

Jeshua must have had a supernatural power latent in

his being. Finding his body is more significant than the body of a significant historical figure or a religious relic. Interested parties might want to find out what his power was and whether it still exists in his remains. What would be the effect of this being true? What would it mean today to the worldwide power brokers and their military?

CONTENTS

PREFACE

CHAPTER ONE:
THE DISCOVERY...11

CHAPTER TWO:
THE THIRTEENTH SCROLL..21

CHAPTER THREE:
THE JUDAS GOAT..52

CHAPTER FOUR:
THE GOLAN HEIGHTS GAMBIT..70

CHAPTER FIVE:
PROJECT 2517..85

CHAPTER SIX:
THE SECOND SCROLL...93

CHAPTER SEVEN:
THE DARK HORSE RISING..102

CHAPTER EIGHT:
THE HEART OF DARKNESS...126

CHAPTER NINE:
UNEXPECTED ALLIANCES...122

CHAPTER TEN:
UNHOLY ALLIANCES..146

CHAPTER ELEVEN:
THE ECLIPSE OF LIGHT AND DARK...................................161

EPILOGUE:
THE RESURRECTION QUESTION...180

Late on a Friday night in his hotel room after an exhausting day, Associate Professor of Neolithic and Bronze Age Archeology David Cross rubbed his tired eyes burning from the daily dose of dust and wind. He was the latest in a line of Oxford scholars starting in 1970 to dig Old Kandahar, founded by Alexander the Great in 330 BCE. Long hours were necessary to pour over his notes and begin the much-needed organization and cataloging of recent finds, none of which had connection to the papyrus scrolls he sought. His years of studying ancient languages went ignored while he fussed over pottery shards, but with hardly any rain and sun every day, even if occasionally ferocious, Kandahar beat Cambridge for weather hands down.

The dig had been difficult due to the local factions, and expected in Afghanistan. Pashtuns followed Pashtunwali, an ethical code that called for being a good host, or were Sunni Muslims who defended their religion at every opportunity. Despite his credentials, the suspicious Sunnis saw David as a spy for the Shiite rebels along the border.

Open notebook pages blurred before he could read them. David knew it was time to stop. The half-empty bottle of bourbon on the table provided by the hotel as a desk seemed to loom toward him. One drink would not be enough. His body ached for relief, making a formidable argument for tipping the bourbon into his tin camp cup. As he struggled with his craving, his cell phone rang. David scrambled to retrieve it from his jacket hanging over the chair, and glanced at the caller's name thinking to let it ring. Long-distance from Rome was important to answer, especially his dear friend and colleague, Mary Russo, from her office at the Museo Egizio, on a study sabbatical from the British Museum. Whip-smart, said her professors; formidable, said the Museum board; uncompromising, said her former boyfriends. Her drive and passion for archeology had landed her the post of Head of Conservation, Conservation and Scientific Research Division.

"David, are you there?"

For a moment her voice sounded distant and unfamiliar. His mind drifted as though he had forgotten the phone in his hand. A whining, irritating buzz scrambled his thoughts. The sound stopped and conscious clarity returned.

"Mary? It's been so long. I'm glad to hear from you."

She hesitated before asking in her melodious voice, "How is the work going?"

Compelled to reassure her, he rushed to answer but lacked a certain conviction.

"Fine, a bit worn around the edges after another

long day at the dig. What have I done to deserve a call from a dear friend?" David tried to sound cheery, but the attempt was blunted by his Oxford stiffness.

She answered with idle chitchat and brought him up to date on her department. David quickly grew weary of the banter. Mary's call out of the blue at this hour seemed odd. Something was being said, hidden behind banality. He wanted more out of her rambling and not in the mood for her games. It was nice to hear her voice, a little irritating but still nice. This was her pattern, to encourage participation in the conversation. Her teasing was a trait that had annoyed him during their too-brief affair at Oxford. She had to have control of every situation and usually did. Her game of cat and mouse was a precursor to leading David where she wanted him. Her beguiling voice made his irritation fall away and soothed him. He pressed her with impatience only to fall back in retreat with a gentler approach.

"Could you please tell me what's on that capacious mind of yours?"

Mary fell quiet for a moment, a little startled at David's frankness. He used to be more patient. Maybe his career had flat-lined, the golden youth of promise stuck in mid-thirties drudgery. She continued to be evasive, and then dropped the pretense.

"Something wonderful has happened and I don't want to discuss it over an open line. Can you break away and come to Rome? I am so excited and I wanted to share the good news with a colleague who could appreciate the situation. You were the first person that came to mind."

"My, we are being particularly mysterious. I might have plans."

"Kandahar was picked clean of anything major years ago and you're single again, have been since you were turned down for a full professorship. Pouting, are we?"

"Point made. My life is somewhat barren at the moment. What about getting out of here?"

"The Museum will make excuses to the faculty. They have to do what we say. David, you must come to Rome straightaway. It's rather urgent. Don't make me plead like a damsel in distress."

"All right, missy. I'll get the next flight out of Kandahar and try to be there by mid-afternoon tomorrow. Will that do? I have a chit around for a compassionate leave airline ticket. Packing should be brief."

She sighed with relief and followed with a reinforcing plea. "Oh yes, that will be fine. Do come, won't you?"

His curiosity was piqued and she ended the call, leaving him to fill the space with his thoughts.

He packed an overnight bag in a hurry and ran out the door with it slamming shut behind him. The elevator was busy. He bolted down the stairwell into the lobby and stepped outside to flag down a ride. To his left, a taxi waited down the street. David's language skills were stuck around the fourth century, modern Pashto beyond him. He said "airport" and waited for a positive response. The driver nodded, turned around in his seat to open the back door, and took off as David settled inside. He checked his bag to make sure he had a clean set of clothes, toothbrush and shaving gear, and his notebook to complete his thoughts and conclusions about the dig during the overnight flight to Rome.

He got aboard with only one seat available. The plane was an old twin engine DC-3 left over from the previous century no doubt and amenities were sparse, only black coffee to drink. It was the only plane leaving that night. Settling back in his seat, he relaxed to the roar of the prop engines revving for takeoff. Then he pulled out his notebook and went through the lists of fragments from Old Kandahar. Mary was right, not a damn missing piece for anyone's puzzle among them.

The drone of the engines put him to sleep and when the plane landed in Ankara to refuel, he found his notebook had fallen from his lap to the floor. Good place for it, he groused. The ground crew wasted no time in prepping the aircraft for takeoff again to his final destination, the Leonardo Da Vinci-Fiumicino airport in Rome.

His weariness from the long hours at the dig took its toll. A deeper sleep overtook him until the plane landed to the north of Terminal 3. He stood on the tarmac with the other passengers and flight crew waiting for the shuttle to the terminal. The sky above Rome was overcast and threatened rain. He anticipated a real shower with hot and cold running water.

Mary waved him down as he left customs through the swinging doors. He was happy to see her. His first impression after five years: she had changed little. She had cut her brown hair long on one side, fashionable enough with her own sense of style. A man he didn't recognize stood beside her, young with black hair obscuring his eyes, and a beard of five days growth. The dashing and adventurous type, David supposed, and had pangs of jealousy or envy.

He approached Mary and her companion ran in front to snap David's overnight bag from his tired grip. He wanted to resist the bold maneuver, but was tired from the long flight.

Mary introduced him as Charles Osgood, a colleague. She wriggled her arm beneath David's as she beamed and kissed him on the cheek. He returned the favor with a dry smile. "Nice reception," he said. "I hope we have time to get Osgood a haircut."

She ushered David out of the terminal as Charles disappeared into the mass of people in front of them. He looked for him with light paranoia about his bag. Sensing his discomfort, Mary assured David he would take good care of his belongings.

He interrupted her. "Reliable sort, eh? My notebook gets nicked and he goes back to the orphanage where you adopted him."

"No worries, he's looking for a ride. He does try to please."

Charles rejoined them with the news of finding a taxi. Mary told the driver they were off to the Musio Egizio on Via Omera. David got in complaining. "I need to shower and clean up."

"Plenty of time for that later, possum. I want you to see what we have."

"What is so urgent? The pleasure of working in antiquities is time never matters."

"This is different from our run of the mill finds. You'll see soon enough."

Turning the key, Mary unlocked the opaque glass door to the anonymous room. The smell rushed into David's nostrils, a stale odor reminiscent of the Egyptian tombs he had been in. He coughed to clear his breathing passages.

David and Charles wandered through the dark and toward the large, oblong flat table sprawled in front of him. It dominated the room. Mary switched on the dim overhead lights, barely illuminating several papyrus scrolls unraveled on the table. The odor increased as David walked forward. It was the scrolls emitting the foul odor.

"Harsh light is bad for the scrolls," Mary explained.

"I've worked with them before or you wouldn't have called me. You need to do something about the air quality in here."

She frowned with disapproval at his remark.

"What's to see, missy? These Qumran scrolls have been studied for years. What is so special?"

"These are from different urns, but have hidden markings in the same hand as far as we can tell. They appear ordinary until exposed to a specific frequency of ultraviolet light."

"That's always done to analyze the authenticity and commonality of the markings. I need more to go on."

"Charles used a battery-powered unit to make sure minimum damage would be done to the papyrus from the unreliable power sources in our building. The battery was low on charge one night, and this caused the UV frequency to shift. That's when we discovered something remarkable."

"Now I am interested. What's remarkable?"

Mary continued with rising excitement, "In the lower portion of one scroll were additional markings not visible with normal UV or regular light. Other scrolls had the same when we tested them. It appears to be ancient Farsi. Collate the markings in the proper order and they represent a coded message."

David leaned on the table and stared at the scrolls. "Have you deciphered the message yet?"

"We are still working on the problem, and that's where you come in, possum," Mary said with hesitation, and then smiled. "Charles and I analyzed the frequency shift of the UV and he rigged a special lamp. That's what we've been using ever since." He paused, biting his lower lip. "Have you told anybody else?"

"Only you."

He scratched his head for a moment. "I don't know. It's been years since I translated root derivations of Farsi and its dialects. My post-doctorate work on the same subject, if you remember, turned into a paper and published in a scrappy little rag."

Mary nodded. "Modesty has never been your strong suit. The 'rag' was the Journal of Archeological Science, and, yes, I still have a copy. Help us decipher the message. Charles and I believe the secret is meant only for initiates. Of what, we are still trying to find out. The markings could be the find of a lifetime."

"The question is who would do this. I mean, go through such trouble. Could be Essenes, Gnostics, or an unknown sect of monks that have escaped notice."

Mary nodded to affirm his conclusions. "With your help, we can uncover who and where and why. What do you say?"

David looked at Charles, then to Mary. He smiled. "Okay I'm in. Old Kandahar may never forgive me. When do we start?"

Mary responded, "Now."

David considered the obstacles: In the first place, the scrolls Mary had were a minor sampling of those found in Qumran, which made the task more difficult. He asked her where Museo's scrolls fit in with the rest of them. The original find in Cave 1 yielded seven scrolls and by the time ten more caves were excavated, the number of scrolls and fragments reached 972.

"Research shows theft played a major role in their history. Locals burned some of them by mistake, just to keep warm."

David shuddered. "I have toiled on second-rate digs for so long, holding so much history in your hands and using it to fight the chill of a cold desert night sounds like the worst obscenity."

"We make up for their error by being rational and objective scientists, and trace the scrolls and follow the routes. The discovery began with the seven in 1946 and continued for ten years through the other caves. As scrolls appeared, they were smuggled out of the country and many disappeared for years. Since their reemergence, not every one has been recovered. Rumors of private collectors and trading on the black market, while others ended up in the Egyptian Museum of Berlin, and France, and even the Vatican."

"So far, the UV light scans of our scrolls has

exposed strange, almost Coptic, markings. The language is not Aramaic, and the visible writing is without a doubt Hebrew. My guess at this point is it could be Sumerian, or perhaps Akkadian. The problem is the message is incomplete and other scrolls likely contain what is missing. We have pieces of pieces, and no idea where to begin."

Mary shrugged her shoulders. "We must get more. Someone has them: researchers, translators, the gamut of scholars."

"They work with photos instead of originals. Of the scrolls available, who has the greatest collection?"

"The Vatican should," Charles piped in. "Mary, you had a call from that cardinal a couple of weeks ago, what's his name, Antonio."

"Cardinal Alderone," she said. "Benito is his first name. He asked about scrolls, their intrinsic and historical value, what they needed in terms of lighting, humidity, care and handling."

"You told me later he said they were brought into the Vatican Library through a back entrance in the middle of the night."

Mary looked pensive. "Yes, but he made jokes about the circumstances and laughed about the Vatican being involved in nefarious activity. I thought he was kidding around."

"But what if," Charles pressed, "he did witness unnamed, unaccounted scrolls being stored in the library. He had a reason to be suspicious because of how they were obtained."

"Your imagination has the better of you and the whole idea is preposterous."

"It's a bit of a stretch, but say they wanted the acquisition kept quiet."

"Look, Charles, I tried calling back and according to his secretary, Cardinal Alderone is rarely in his office. He is impossible to pin down on any given day. He visits other parishes and attends functions like a political troubleshooter for the Pope."

"What kind of troubleshooter?"

"Priests are under greater scrutiny about sexual abuse, and when a case is made public he rushes in to quiet the press and provide defense. The cardinal is in the news making statements about denying the allegations."

Charles smacked his lips. "That's perfect. Mary, ring him up and say you have damning evidence against the bishop of East Anglia, an Ordinary with extra. He would take that call."

"That is quite enough. You have exceeded past the furthest reach of propriety, and I will not be a part of such a harebrained and illegal scheme." Charles pursued. "Think of what it could mean to have more of the elusive message."

"I couldn't lie to Cardinal Alderone. He is a priest, no matter how snaky, and a cardinal." She glared at Charles and turned to David for sympathy.

"I have the least religious leanings in archeology, missy," he said. "Abusing a priest's trust is out of my line, besides sinning against a sinner doesn't make a sin, or worthy of excommunication. My faith lies in science, real live substantiated facts I can sink my teeth into, but I try to stay on the right side of ecclesiastics in case I need to confess on my deathbed."

Mary grimaced. "David, you were a coward in Oxford, always slinking around with your tawdry affairs, never giving a thought to the poor girls. You are still a spineless plonker."

"My job often involves charging into dark caves, facing unsavory curses and threats of an unsavory death when I open a tomb. So much for your insult. A true coward stays at home reading Howard Carter."

"I am sorry, possum. That was uncalled for, but you never stood by me when I had to fight Oxford sexism for my full professorship. Be on my side for once."

"Sorry, missy. I was never interested in chivalry, that Sir Gawain and the Green Knight, Walter

Raleigh hogwash. I play with others the best I know how. Maybe not getting involved is a character flaw, but it's who I am.

"You are at a loss of what to do. This is a stalemate. I need more of the marked scrolls to find the prime word to unlock this mess. There simply isn't enough text for anything."

Mary squirmed. "All right, you win. I'll do it."

"How?" Charles challenged. "Skullduggery or the direct approach?"

Mary responded. "I'll send a letter alluding to problems in East Anglia. That should encourage his response."

"Takes too long. The cardinal's people might regard it as a prank and ignore you," said David.

"I can leave a veiled, yet sincerely troubled request with the secretary."

"Early, before afternoon lethargy sets in. Since this is settled, we should lock up," suggested David.

"It's two in the morning and nothing else can be done. Besides, this working into the wee hours has cut into my beauty sleep."

"And mine as well, David. Rest should put us to rights for a fresh start." She headed toward the door.

"Charles, get us a taxi to our hotel. Don't forget to switch off the lights on your way out."

The three conspirators rejoined in the scroll room

at the Museo shortly after sunrise. David had trouble getting any sleep. Given how the others looked, they also suffered from the same malady. Mary left her message with the office of Cardinal Alderone while stirring non-dairy creamer into her single cup of coffee for the day.

They sat at the table of scrolls. The room was quiet except for the hum from the building air conditioner. Warm air pungent with the odor from the scrolls surrounded them, and silence lay like a blanket. One by one they took turns disturbing the stillness by getting a cup of coffee or another gulp from the water cooler. Those mundane distractions circled Mary's cell phone.

Then came a ring that pierced their ears with an incongruous joyful staccato. Mary picked up her cell expecting to hear the cardinal's voice, but it was only the assistant keeper of the late antique Egyptian division confirming the arrival of a decorated bowl unearthed at the Valley of the Kings dig, on loan from the Museum of Egyptian Antiquities in Cairo.

"Glad to hear about the bowl. Interrupting a sabbatical is not a treasonable offense as long as the signed paperwork is sent off before lunch so we stay on good terms with Cairo. Thank you, Evelyn." She set the cell down, a relief from the overwhelming tension of expectation.

***

At the Vatican, Cardinal Renaldo Pila returned from a private audience with Pope Clement XV. Pila, a fusty old man with greased-down white hair and dust on his soutane, oversaw the library archives in a section of the building that few of the clergy had seen.

The subject of discussion was the acquisition of important documents from World War II on the failure of Church policy, along with a number of Qumran scrolls that had recently become available on the black market. These were delivered late at night far from anyone's prying eyes or unsanctioned curiosity. The packages, handled by a broker who had the Vatican's complete confidence, also promised the discretion both parties needed.

The scrolls allegedly contained Jeshua's own words, and troubled the Pope. Jeshua's personal diary and private teachings were given to the twelve disciples, written in Aramaic.

His teachings described a different perspective, opposing an intercessor to God and the need for the priesthood. They bore witness against the apostolic format and challenged the foundation of the Church. The scrolls had to be buried; the College of Bishops and the Vatican itself would explode if the news were made public. Its essence contained revelations that would change the world and disrupt or destroy the faith of the Church's devoted followers around the world. And worse, threaten to dismantle the Church.

The Pope received word of the scrolls through the broker, already having knowledge of the translations, and arranged their purchase for a tidy sum. Clement was prepared to clean out the Vatican coffers to get them.

Once the scrolls were in the Vatican, he ordered the grand master of the Priory of Sion for Rome to hunt down and eliminate the former possessor of the scrolls, as a precaution should he attempt extorting the church later. The Priory was regarded as a fringe group, but steadfast in their protection of the Church. It was founded in France in 1956 and quickly discredited and dissolved, but myths are hard to debunk and the Priory went underground and flourished. The organization came to the attention of the Vatican in the late 1960s; Pope Paul VI enlisted the Priory members as defenders of the faith, passing them on to his successor, Pope John Paul I, who was struck down by the Priory after attempting to disband them. Pope John Paul II had better skill at utilizing their talents and became the grand master's confessor.

The Pope ordered the scrolls stored among other artifacts considered dangerous and obscured from public view, buried deep inside the archives. Cardinal Pila had sole responsibility and Cardinal Alderone was the only member of the clergy allowed entrance.

Alderone had spent the day before in a meeting with Bishop Montague, head of the Southwark diocese at St. George's Cathedral in London, and flying back to Rome. The press was chasing the bishop about his questionable handling of the protests directed at the behavior of priests in his diocese. Public outcries revealed several instances of misconduct involving youths with a Catholic charity for wayward children in Southwark.

The bishop asked for legal counsel and advice on how to deal with the looming scandal, especially the tabloids. This was Cardinal Alderone's specialty. With an investigation regarding the allegations still underway, his priorities were to stave off more assaults by the media and make sure Montague did not speak to reporters out of turn.

Cardinal Alderone arrived at his office in the afternoon with Mary's message waiting for his attention. Charles was right about the reaction. Alarmed by another problem in the same city, he called Mary immediately.

In the scroll room, Mary and David were tired of waiting and planned to go out for lunch. Charles would stay behind with Mary's cell phone. No sooner had they reached the door than Charles called out, "Mary, wait! Your call just came through."

Mary placed her hand against the closing door, her heart beating. She looked at David with desperation. He put his hand on her shoulder. "You'll be fine, missy. Stay focused and keep the details vague."

She nodded with a lump in her throat and walked across the room to take her cell from Charles. He whispered, "He sounds agitated, so be strong and righteous."

"This is Mary Russo. May I help you?"

"This is Cardinal Benito Alderone. You wanted to speak?"

Mary paused before launching her well-conceived lie. "Thank you for returning my call. I felt you should know about a matter that has come to my attention."

"What is this about, my dear?" Alderone returned.

"A friend reached out to me with great distress about her son, Lawrence. She was adamant I not reveal her identity and Lawrence is not his real name. According to my friend, a priest in East Anglia made sexual advances on her son. The local diocese is doing nothing. I didn't know what to do when I remembered our conversation. If anyone knew of an action to be taken, it would be you."

Mary pressed on. "Because of the flap in the news regarding St. George's, you wouldn't want another problem in East Anglia. My friend is open to an arrangement, a settlement, to avoid casting more shame on the Church. Perhaps we should meet to discuss this?"

"I understand. Where did you have in mind?"

"Near the Museo is a café at the Valle Giulia light rail station. It's not frequented much, so we could enjoy privacy."

"I have important matters that need my attention. Let us say around four this afternoon. What is the name of this café?"

"It's called 'Mangia Roma.' Not very original, but they serve a nice strawberry tart when the fruits are in season."

"Until we meet. Ciao, Signorina Russo."
Mary cut the connection and sighed in relief. "That's that."

"Now comes the tough part, closing the deal," said Charles. "Offer to keep quiet about the affair without compensation, then say your friend has left London, and trade your silence for access to the Vatican Library for a look at the scrolls."

Mary was dubious about her ability to carry out the treachery.

"Remember, you are not a woman of questionable morals, only an actress standing on the stage of deceit, vying for something remarkable in the name of science."

Mary looked at Charles with her eyes glazed. "Wow, Osgood old chap is really excited about putting you in harm's way. Will he don armor and sit astride a white horse to defend your honor? I don't think so," David giggled.

"That's quite enough. Charles is trying to make a contribution. What are you doing?" chided Mary.

"I am studying the photographs of what we have, and giving my curiosity its head to solve the meaning and purpose behind the markings. I want my hands on the Vatican scrolls."

With a little over two hours before meeting with Alderone, Mary tried to keep busy by reading the proof sheets of the latest catalogue. Time was unkind and moved slow for everyone.

"Charles," she said, "The coffee shop is a fifteen minute walk from here. I should be late, no more than five minutes, to help put the cardinal at an emotional disadvantage by raising his anxiety."

Charles and David agreed and praised her suggestion as proactive.

Mary put on a dark blue topcoat to cloak her appearance as an astute scientist. Charles added to her apparel, a St. Christopher medal his mother had given him when he left home to attend university. He placed it around her neck and shortened the chain so it was visible.

"St. Christopher has been demoted or de-sanctified, hasn't he?" asked Mary.

"Would never dream of giving you an out-of-date saint. His feast day clogged the universal liturgical calendar and removed for lack of space. He is still a saint and worshipped as such," said Charles.

"How embarrassing. I'm not Catholic, and barely an Evangelical through my father."
She stood across from Mangia Roma waiting for the cardinal to enter, and stayed for five minutes after his arrival. This allowed time for him to find a comfortable place to sit and the calculated anxiety at her lateness to set in.

Mary saw Alderone seated near the back, partially obscured by the counter where one other patron was sitting. Catching his impatience, she nodded and smiled at him. She walked to his lonely booth and slid across the seat in front of him, keeping her eyes on his troubled face.

"Shall we get on with it?" she asked.
The Cardinal squirmed in his seat and he nodded

to continue. He clasped his hands with fingers locked together on the table in prayer. His eyes noticed the medallion perched on bare throat above her blouse, and made him relax. The old school religion showed in her choice of saint. "You are of the Catholic faith, I see. Tell me what's this all about?"

Mary leaned forward and said, "Father, my friend has taken her son and left London to avoid any further involvement. Reports from St. George's put quite the fright into her, how the boys are cast as reprobates when the priests are at fault. However, since I am privy to her plight and your responsibilities, I wish to propose a special request. Details of what happened in East Anglia must be kept private for everyone's sake, especially the boy. He told his mother what the priest asked of him, shocking, reprehensible acts for a man of the cloth."

The cardinal's eyes narrowed and a furrow formed on his brow. Despite this, he remained stone-faced and glared at her boldness, disarming her and ending any further assault.

"Extortion is a mortal sin, Signorina Russo. I would be careful. You are treading on dangerous spiritual ground."

Mary returned his nasty volley. "I'm not the one seeking to avoid a public scandal, Father. I can go to the press with what I know. I don't think you want that, do you?"

Cardinal Alderone squeezed his hands, which s ettled into prayer position as he capitulated to the strength of her words. "What do you have in mind?"

Mary spoke with even more confidence to pursue her prey. "When you contacted me about archival conditions for ancient scrolls, my guess is the scrolls in question are from the Qumran dig. The archeological community knows of the Vatican's interest in obtaining the scrolls from any source. Is this true?"

The cardinal blanched. "Part of the Vatican's mission is continued study of historical parchments and papyrus to further understand the beginnings of our religion."

"Let's not waste each other's time. Out of the entire find, a small percentage of the scrolls and fragments concerned religious matters. The Museo Egizio has a few currently on loan, and the rest are either in your possession or reported to be missing. I want to see what you have, and so do two of my colleagues."

"Not possible."

"Look, we are scientists trying to establish a history of the scrolls. We need to see what you have to bolster what we already know in our research. You can arrange for this in any clandestine manner you wish. Isn't that what you do, guide the faithful by clever misdirection?"

The cardinal shrugged in acknowledgement. "You must understand I'm not in charge of antiquities. Cardinal Pila is my senior and he would not approve."

"He need not be told. Besides, what he doesn't know he cannot refuse."

"What you ask is difficult and perhaps impossible. The archive is always locked. I do not have the keys."

"Bosh. Really, Cardinal, the man known as the Pope's troubleshooter has trouble with locked doors?"

"Certain times I am given the keys to the archive for safekeeping, as when Cardinal Pila goes on other church matters for a few days."

"Perfect," said Mary. "When will this Pila fellow be going out of town?"

Cardinal Alderone became pensive. "I'm not privy to his schedule. Sometimes I'm told right before he has to leave."

"When you find out, call me and I will be there."

"Entrance must be at night to draw less attention and dismantle the alarm system. You cannot come through the Library. That is locked after a certain hour. You should travel through another passage where there are no guards."

Mary smiled. "Simple, dear Cardinal, provide us with an escort to drive us from our hotel to Vatican City. Blindfold us if you wish and lead us to the scrolls. We leave how we entered and your secrets remain so."

Cardinal Alderone wore a troubled look. "I'm not sure about this."

"My team will be in and out before anyone knows."

"Wait for me. In the meantime, stay away from further blackmail schemes and for God's sake, attend a mass for the sake of your damaged soul."
Mary rose from the booth satisfied with the bargain struck between them. She left first, with Alderone escaping shortly after.

Inside the scroll room, triumph freshened the thick air.

"The deal is done," Mary declared.

"Amazing. I didn't know whether you would pull this off. Congratulations," said David.

"Good job, Mary," said Charles. "When do we go?"

Mary frowned. "Wait for Alderone. He will let us know when it can happen. Don't worry, he'll call when the time is set."

The cell rang before the empty wrappers from takeout dinners had been cleared from a card table. Mary picked up her phone and whispered shush to David and Charles. "Hello, this is Mary Russo, can I help you?"

"It will be tomorrow. I have ordered a car to collect you at the Hotel Prati on Via Crescenzio. This is your address, yes? An escort will come at six p.m. I'll be waiting in Vatican City," the cardinal murmured.

Mary cut the connection. "We're on, gentlemen."

The two connecting rooms at the Hotel Prati were small, inexpensive, uncomfortable, and the perfect location for tourists: the Vatican, Centro Storico, Castle St. Angelo, and Trastevere in walking distance. Mary looked at her watch, gritted her teeth, and stiffened with impatience. David cursed the cramped bathroom while two car-horn honks sounded from the street below. Charles checked the gear in his duffle bag, making sure nothing appeared strange or dubious when they arrived.

David reached for the duffle bag. "I have this." Charles followed behind him and Mary picked up the rear. She stared at the silly truncated room for a moment, and wondered if they would return, then with grim determination she closed the door.

A young man wearing a black visor cap sat at the

wheel of a dark BMW sedan with smoked windows. He held the rear door open for his passengers, grunted when he was greeted, and handed back three sleep masks. "Put on now. All we could find," he said.

The route taken to Vatican City was made labyrinthian by the driver, full of twists and turns not seen on any map. Once inside the City, what should have been a straight line along Stradone dei Giardini or Via Pio X turned into a crooked approach the passengers could only guess at. Mary knew from studying a map earlier that slightly northeast of St. Peter's Basilica stood the Apostolic Palace; north across the Belvedere Courtyard past museums was their goal, the Vatican Apostolic Library.

They stripped off the sleep masks when told and climbed out of the BMW: Mary first, then Charles, with David the last after sliding across the seat with the duffle bag in hand. The duffle bag made David's exit difficult. Charles offered his help, but David held his palm flat to show no help needed.

The driver motioned for them to follow him close to the wall until they reached a thick door made of rough-cut timbers and secured by iron hinges. Its knocker had the face of a half-lion/half-man with its mouth gaped as though it were screaming. High points exposed unpolished brass beneath the blackening. The door had the striking resemblance of a gate leading into a medieval castle, with a knight sporting a full set of armor waiting on the other side. Construction on the Apostolic Castle dated from the sixteenth century and made this less unlikely than it should have been.

By now it was dark outside. But inside beyond the door the Courtyard of the Library shone under the lanterns mounted on the inner walls. The courtyard was well manicured with green grass cut short. Several stone footpaths led in different directions.

Cardinal Alderone waited for his interlopers and called for them to follow. He led them to a door looking much more modern, and with an arch at the top and small stained glass window illuminated by a warm interior light. The cardinal pulled a set of keys from under his soutane, unlocked the door to a marble-floored anteroom with a spiral staircase winding down to a lower level.

The staircase seemed to go on forever. At the bottom a set of dark oak doors covered the special archives, unknown and separated from the Vatican Library. Alderone opened the doors sideways to reveal a large room with thirty-foot high ceilings. Walls of shelves with different-sized niches divided the space that held magnificent artifacts.

Alderone turned left and preceded along an aisle between the walled shelves. Just before they reached their destination, David glanced to his right at an astonishing sight. Suspended on a backboard before him was the lance of Longinus, the infamous "Spear of Destiny," used by a Roman soldier to pierce the side of Jeshua at the crucifixion site. Thought lost to the world, mused David, yet it hangs under Vatican City.

He poked Mary to catch her attention and pointed to the lance. Her eyes widened, and she whispered, "I wonder what else is here no one knows about?"

Alderone halted in front of a temperature-and humidity-controlled cabinet at the end of the aisle. Inside were twenty scrolls, wrapped in dried leather and stacked like loaves of bread. He waited until the three stood close to him and said, "These are what you are after. You know how to treat them, as ours are more delicate than yours." He pointed to a long table across the aisle from where they stood.

"Use that for your work. May I remind you, you have a limited time of two hours. I will show you out when you are to leave."

He looked at Mary and she nodded in agreement. She whispered, "Thank you, Cardinal, you've been very gracious."

They wasted little time. David placed the papyrus

scrolls side by side on the table while Charles pulled equipment from the duffle bag. He stopped to consider the scrolls and shook his head. "This is like Christmas morning."

"We can't examine every one with the attention they deserve. Let's photograph as much as we can, then we can feast on these beauties when we get back to the Museo."

David unrolled the scrolls while Charles took infrared and ultraviolet photos. Mary helped with the scrolls and waited for Cardinal Alderone to show up at any minute.

The trio labored feverishly to accomplish the task at hand. They were on the last two scrolls when a knock on the door put a halt to their endeavors. The door locked from inside and only the keys carried by the cardinal could open it. They held their breath as someone called out to Alderone.

"Cardinal Alderone, is everything all right?" Lights in the room must have been seen from outside. Another knock sounded. They dared not make a sound and hoped whoever was looking for Alderone would soon give up. Then muffled voices, one of them possibly belonged to Alderone.

Loud exchanges between the voices sputtered to a moment of silence before the lock turned. The door swung open and revealed Cardinal Alderone appearing quite disgruntled. "I hope you have concluded your business. It is time to leave. I convinced Cardinal Baldini that I had left the lights on. I assured him I would extinguish them as soon as I finished my rounds."

Charles assured the cardinal they had two scrolls left to scan and would soon be out of his hair. Cardinal Alderone hissed, "Be quick about it."

"Won't take but a moment," said Charles.

Alderone turned to look beyond the staircase and confirm no one else were coming, and Charles snapped the last photos.

"David, help me return the scrolls to their homes on the shelves," said Mary.

He gathered several, while Charles shoved cameras and lights into the duffle bag.

"Let's go find our driver, shall we?" said Mary.

Charles closed the bag and swung it over his shoulder. Mary headed for the door and David stayed close behind with Charles at his heels. They walked behind the cardinal paying little attention to his presence. Mary bounded the stairs two at a time and so did David, but Charles only ambled with the burden of the duffle bag weighing him down. She whispered to Charles, "Come on, lad, are you waiting on the tram?"

"Yes, mum. Right away, mum," he grumbled.

They stayed in the cardinal's wake and moved through the courtyard as though well-established tenants. The driver waited by the car with the sleep masks in hand.

"Same rules to get out as get in," he said.

Mary was the first in the back seat and last to leave at the Hotel Prati. They stood outside in the shadow of the hotel sign for a moment feeling relieved.

"Missy, did we just pull a stunt on the Holy See, the Vatican and its Library, and every God-fearing believer in the western world?"

"Yes we did, possum, and a bagatelle in my opinion. The religious types take themselves too seriously."

After less sleep than any of them wanted, the trio was at the Museo Egizio. David gazed at the slabs and boxes of cast concrete and glass of the building rise and tower before them. Mary unlocked the scroll room, and each plopped down into the nearest chair they could find. Charles dropped his duffle bag to the floor, caring little about its contents.

"Easy with that bag. Our future lies in it," chided Mary.

The cameras were state-of-the-art digital, with the frames only needing to be uploaded on the computer for a better look. "I'm up for a fresh cup of coffee before starting the tech work," he said. "Any takers?"

"Had enough coffee to keep me awake into the weekend, but I could use a stiff drink. Is there anything stronger available, missy?"

Mary chortled. "Certainly, good possum. We archeologists are notorious for taking advantage of duty-free liquor."

They laughed together.

A bottle of bourbon was found and passed around along with paper cups. Mary swallowed her shot like a true Oxonian. Charles sipped at his and David set his cup down empty.

"I realize it's late, but I'm game to go at our spoils right now," said Mary. "Charles, can you get us on screen?"

Charles stared into his cup. "Hardly any sleep and drinking before lunch does not make for optimal conditions, but what the hell? I signed on for the long hours."

"I'm still jazzed about our escapade, so let's make use of that energy," said David.

Mary jumped from her chair to the equipment spread on the table. "I took the liberty of having a large monitor desktop transferred here. We can connect to the Museo's mainframe for whatever memory or access we need."

Charles picked up the keyboard while David swept the scrolls aside.

"Let's see what we have for our troubles," said Mary.

"With the FireWire connections from the infrared camera, you should be able to upload now," said David.

Mary typed on the keyboard and hit the enter button. "I've set the desktop to upload what Charles took in sequence, so we should see the frames appear soon."

They watched the monitor for the results until the beep with an error prompt. Mary turned pale. David looked over her shoulder and noticed an oversight.

"Missy, the photo rendering is set for normal spectrum rendering."

"Damn you, possum. You're right. Good catch."

"I'm here to help."

Mary entered "file render." Several choices popped up and she chose "infrared," and tapped "enter."

The computer beeped with a message to "standby for rendering infrared data files." A rapid set of pulses and the first frame unfolded.

"Sorry for the slow speed," Mary apologized. "The firmware is over a year old and waiting to be upgraded. This might take a little longer than we expected."

"I'm in no hurry as long as it works," said David. "Besides it gives me the opportunity to dip into the bourbon one more time."

"Be my guest, you deserve it. Here's the first shot of scroll number 1. Doesn't look too bad."

Charles peered at the monitor. "The picture should be sharper."

"My fault. The display is usually set at a lower resolution to make regular office documents read faster. That's easy to fix." She halted the rendering program to reset in high definition, and then resumed the scanning process.

"Later we can alter the rendering to change detail and contrast when we find what we want."

David sipped his second drink and sat the bottle of aged bourbon down on an open side counter. "Sounds good."

Mary had her eyes transfixed on the computer screen. "Damn, I wish I this process went faster. I will be retired and a grandmother before these frames download properly."

"Fear not," said David. "You're almost at the half way mark. We can view each frame on full screen when you are finished loading."

"You're right. I'm just so damn eager to get a better look."

"These are only renditions of the infrared. I'm anticipating the UV versions. Will we find other fragments of the code on the Vatican's scrolls? I hope so. I'd hate to think we went through that cloak and dagger business for nothing."

"Not all is lost. We have more scrolls to savor." David grunted. "I'm not interested in the text, just the code."

With the pictures finally loaded, Mary called up the first frame in full screen mode and translated the Aramaic. "Charles, David, you've got to see this. I can't believe what I am reading."

David rushed over, drink in hand, with Charles at his heels. "Found the amazing and heretical, missy?"

Mary indicated the lines with her finger: "It says Jeshua is talking to Peter in this line, and he says, 'this is my wife Mary, she is also my disciple.' In the next line Jeshua says, 'I have taught her more than you because she is closer than all of you.'"

She stopped, shocked and pensive. "Can this be true? If these documents are authenticated, this could dismantle the Church." Mary went on to another frame. "This one says, and Jeshua is still talking, 'if you look under a rock, I am there. If you look under a tree stump, I am there, believe when I say, there is no intercessor between man and God.'"

Mary fell into her chair. "Do you realize what this

means? This undermines the whole apostolic foundation of the priesthood."

"The Church acquired these scrolls to keep them from the prying eyes of the public," said Charles. "They should stop at nothing to keep them secret, yet let us examine them to avoid another scandal. Someone in Rome is falling down on the job."

Mary nodded in agreement.

David said, "The text in these scrolls is hot only if translated by an acknowledged expert."

Mary scowled. "You know how many years I spent studying Aramaic with my father."

"A better man never walked in shoe leather. I was only playing the devil's advocate and meant no disrespect. We have evidence of the Church's chicanery. Change the rendering to UV and see if you can find our precious markings."

Mary entered the program for resetting the rendering format. She touched the enter button and the first frame came up without markings visible on the screen. David looked over her shoulder with anticipation.

He slumped and declared with frustration, "Oh, that's just great."

"Relax, David. Some of the other scrolls didn't have the markings. Besides, there are many more frames to look at."

"May I sit in the driver's seat so I can see for myself?"

"Sure. Have a go."

David shifted to the next frame. A smile grew across his face, "Ah, there's one." Continuing to peruse the frames, he logged twelve more with markings. Staring at the screen for a few moments, he soon had every appearance of the markings copied on a separate file.

David gasped with delight. Mary standing across the room replied, "What?"

Charles rushed over to stand behind David, looking over his shoulder with bewilderment at the file David had created. "Can you make any sense out of this gibberish?"

"I think I have the primer," said David. "A primer is a single word that becomes the primary key to the others, in this case establishes the word order. This is very exciting. Now if I bring in the markings from the other scrolls and apply the primer, they rotate and form a matrix. The rest is a matter of translating the ancient Farsi."

David took out his notebook and jotted down corresponding words from what he had before. His eyes widened as he made sense of the messages they contained.

"We may have another missing papyrus or

parchment, a thirteenth scroll. It's not in Qumran. There is a map of what appears to be Cairo, but the city was founded in 968. Makes no sense on a first century scroll."

"David," Mary asked. "Have you ever heard of marginalia, those notes scholars write in the margins of books? At any time in one thousand years the scrolls might have been taken up and studied, and the writing applied."

"Sure, but the dating of the scrolls give us no reason to believe they were moved."
"Dating remains the same regardless. I imagine whoever had responsibility for the scrolls moved them frequently to escape destruction or discovery. Can you be more specific on the location?"

"Just bring up a map of modern Cairo, the old section."

Mary watched the screen. "It's a backstreet still there. Grab your hats and coats, gentlemen. We're going to Egypt."

The team arrived in Cairo at early evening as the sun was about to set. The sky turned to mauve with deep red highlights, making the view out of the plane's window looking more like a Broadway production.

They deplaned and went to the baggage area. The luggage lie on the ground like an assembly line, forcing them to look at every tag as several bags looked identical.

A taxi arrived in front of the airport with its Mercedes emblem displayed. Mary had booked rooms at the prestigious Oberoi Hotel. When they tried to check in, the night manager said, "Sorry, but we're booked." After much argument, she conceded defeat. The hotel provided accommodations at the smaller less extravagant Berlin Hotel, with its aquamarine walls, green doors, and sun yellow ceilings, one mile from the Khan el-Khalili Bazaar. After they settled in their rooms, the change had made them much closer to their destination.

The flight was more draining than expected. They were exhausted and agreed to begin their search in the morning.

***

In a hovel located deep in the winding storefronts

and shops of Old Cairo sat a small, frail, bearded man. Mohammed Ahmed hunched over his laptop motionless like a stunned beetle, with a working left eye and the right blinded from an explosion near his home, wearing a faded djellaba, a full-body garment worn by Arab men. Held between his parched lips was a half-smoked cigarette dripping with ash.

Mohammed was an informant for the Islamic Gnostic Brotherhood, charged with guarding against outsiders trying to confiscate or steal sacred Egyptian relics. He intercepted Mary's email with the general manager of the conservation department of the Museum of Egyptian Antiquities, Dr. Yasmin Razek. It read as follows: "Found possible evidence of scroll hidden in your city and flying to Cairo with my team. This is an opportunity to discover a new and important artifact for Egypt. See attached file. Will contact you in two days."

Mohammed called Anwar Bushid, leader of the Brotherhood in Cairo. "Asalam Alaykum, Brother Bushid. I think we have a problem. Better meet to decide what we should to do. I fear the sacred thirteenth scroll is in danger of immanent discovery." Anwar answered. "Wa Asalam Alaykum as-Salaam, Brother Ahmed. I understand. I will call a gathering for tonight in the usual place and discuss what to do."

That evening in the small back room of a local coffee house, six members of the Brotherhood sat around a table with three legs. It was hand-carved by a local artisan and cherished by the storekeeper, and bore many prankish children's initials carved into the top to frustrate him.

Glasses of strong coffee sat around the table carrying the aroma of anise, a popular drink among the locals. A tattered bed-sheet drooping over a slackened rope covered the room from the public and added privacy. No one frequented the coffee house at that hour, leaving the group with complete quietness.

"Asalam Alaykum, brothers," Bushid opened. "Thank you for coming on such short notice. Brother Ahmed has brought a matter of extreme importance to my attention. It seems we have clever people on the trail of the thirteenth scroll."

"Wa Asalam Alaykum as-Salaam, Brother Bushid. I thought its whereabouts were cloaked by virtue of the ancient code."

"Yes, we had. It seems someone clever enough to not only identify the language but has also broken the code."

Brother Hasim said, "What can be done at this hour? They are in Cairo and according to our informant know where to look."

"Much to our disappointment we have to create a

violent diversion. We will attack them at their hotel and make it look like jihadists, but first we must move the scroll to a safe location."

Bashid turned to Brother Yasin. "Asalam Alaykum, Brother Bashid. What must I do?"

"My friend, you will obtain the armament to make it appear our violent friends have committed a rival attack. Wait until they leave their hotel in the morning and then launch the rocket-propelled grenade to eliminate them. No one will be wise. This will appear as a grievance against American journalists meddling in Cairo's politics. Insha Allah."

*****

At the Central Intelligence Agency in Langley, Virginia, the Directorate of Support's Office of Information Technology bustled with people flitting from one cubicle to another discussing the movements of nefarious individuals and known terrorist organizations.

Their duties entailed using data collected from several military satellite channels. The monitored communications related to the efforts of violent groups advocating jihad, a holy war against infidels. Plots against the United States and, several targets in other countries in Europe were their main concern.

Computer activity and cell phone usage between various cells represented their primary focus. Next to the intelligence gathered by case officers in the field, a top priority was international cyber crimes.

Bill specialized in cyber crime. He left his station to get a cup of coffee and returned to his computer screen flashing an alert showing suspicious activity detected in Cairo. Bill had been with the Agency for only five weeks, not long enough to be recognized by his last name. He was Bill, just Bill to his superiors.

Bill printed out a screen shot of his computer and rushed to the office of Alexander Colby, a florid, middle-aged man who spent off-hours in the gym fighting the pull of his years, and head of the Directorate for Support. The data seemed peculiar. Bill wanted Colby's advice for the next steps to take. Colby scrutinized the printout. He squirmed behind his gray desk wondering what he had. He puzzled over the language through reading glasses perched low on his nose.

"Have you seen anything like this before?" Colby asked indignantly. Bill shook his head back and forth.

"That's why I brought it straight to you, sir. Usually this guy, I'm assuming it's a man, no information there, sneaks into email accounts of government and cultural leaders, the usual bullshit, excuse me, and gets nothing. This time he scored a photo file full of ancient writing. I thought you'd know what I should do."

Colby grunted approval. He made a brushing off gesture toward Bill, showing it was time to leave his office. Colby knew this was ripe for the cypher boys. He left his office with the printout. With a measured gait he went down the hall, broken only by the abrupt turn toward the elevator. The door closed behind him and he reached for the third-floor button. He headed for Leonard Scalisi, the team leader in charge of the cypher group.

The telephone seemed glued to Scalisi's right ear. He turned to see Colby pressing for his attention. Scalisi raised his index finger to halt the interruption and cupped his hand over the phone. He whispered, "I'll just be a moment."

Impatience let the printout drop on the desk. Scalisi eyed the document in front of him. He told the party on the line, "I'll get right back to you."

"I received this an hour ago," Colby said. "Thought your people could make something of it. Might be important or even a false lead. But I think the bad guys have created a code to get back on the internet."

"Okay. I'll get right on this." Scalisi smiled.

"Don't worry. As soon as I know something, I'll let you know."

Colby left the office breathing easier. Scalisi had single-handed broken the Russian code six years before, allowing the CIA to view sensitive materials pouring out of the Kremlin.

The staff in Colby's office joked that he was a regular bloodhound on his hunches. His nose was always on target. He returned to the fourth floor and stood motionless looking through the closed blinds. The maze of cubicles spread out before him. Though he worried about those unidentified symbols, he was proud of his staff, especially the new boy, Bill. He must find out his last name, give him a leg up.

***

Sunrise was still an hour away, but the team had packed and was ready to travel. Mary took her smaller bag and Charles and David shared the burden of the other two. They exited the hotel lobby and loaded the rented Humvee.

Charles said, "I'll drive while you guide me, Mary."

She nodded in compliance. David threw the last bag in the back and stepped aboard. Without warning, Charles saw the missile's smoke trail headed straight for them. He screamed, "RPG! Quick, get out!"

David had one foot inside, grabbed Mary's arm, and jumped clear. Charles struggled with his safety belt and broke the clasp just as the missile struck the right side of the vehicle, flipping it on its side.

The smoke and flames subsided. Shocked and dazed, David sat in a ditch looking at the wreckage. He called out, "Charles, are you all right?"

There was no answer. David tried to stand but wrenching pain let him know his left leg bore a piece of Humvee door latch in his thigh. He leaned against the curb to see Mary beside him unconscious and bleeding. He shook her, shook her again.

"Missy, speak to me. Come on, girl, give possum a sign."

The blast had stunned her. Mary moved and opened her eyes. "What happened?" She wiped at her face, covered with splattered blood from a gash across her forearm. She cried out.

"It's just a scratch, missy. But I don't see Charles anywhere and I can't stand just yet."

People from the hotel gathered around the wreckage with timid curiosity.

David turned to Mary. "You stay put. I will go for Charles."

He pulled himself to a sitting position, turned

toward the street ahead, and inched past the remains of the vehicle still burning. The baggage was part way open and on fire. "Oh shit," he thought. "There go the cameras." He called for Charles and his voice grew weaker. There was still no answer. David feared Charles was a casualty.

He moved past the rear of the upside-down wreckage and saw a pair of feet without shoes under the vehicle's hood.

"There you are," he said. "Are you awake, or better still, are you alive?"

He listened to a low mumbling from under the hood. It was a meager groan. David reached out. "I'm coming. Have you out of there in a jiffy."

Charles was in bad shape and barely conscious. Soon the Egyptian police arrived on the scene and administered aid to Mary and David while Charles was removed on a stretcher. An ambulance came next. Mary went on a stretcher, bandaged about the head and arm and moved into the first ambulance, just as a second picked up Charles. They had attached an oxygen mask to him along with an IV.

David sat on the curb with a bandage wrapped around his thigh covering the wound the shrapnel had caused. They tended to him last as he was the most conscious. The trio was taken to the Cairo Medical Center on Abou Ebaid El Bakry Street for various tests and treatment.

Young and clean-shaved Dr. Jamal Said entered David's room and took his blood pressure. When he finished, he said. "The police are outside and want to ask you some questions. I have told them their interrogation should be short as you are still in shock."

David thanked the doctor for his concern. "What about my two friends? Are they hurt badly?"

"The sedated woman is resting. She has a concussion, but should recover with time. Her arm suffered deep lacerations that missed her artery. We administered antibiotics while our supplies last.

"The man remains unconscious. There has been abdominal bleeding. We have taken measures to halt this, but his condition is very serious and beyond our ability to administer treatment. He needs to be moved to another hospital, but we cannot do this without written consent. I would suggest the International Medical Center on Ramsis Square."

David interrupted. "I take full responsibility for his care. Please, you must help him right away."

Dr. Said placed his hand on David's shoulder. "All right, we will call for the transfer, but you must sign the papers right away."

"I will sign whatever you need. Just get him the medical care he needs."

***

Several days passed and Dr. Said questioned whether Charles would be better at an intensive care facility in Dubai instead of the International Medical Center. Colleagues had not responded to his frantic emails. David learned to walk with a cane.

Mary was on another floor and David hobbled down the stairs several times to visit her. He watched her sleep from a hallway separated by a glass window. Late in the afternoon of the fourth day he found her sitting up in her bed being fed by a nurse. His heart skipped a beat.

David asked a nurse leaving the ward if he could speak to her. She was reluctant until she saw the worry in his eyes and agreed for a short time. He limped into the ward and her bed. Her eyes were closed, and she opened them when David placed his hand on hers. She smiled.

"Missy, how are you holding up?"

For a moment, she struggled to speak. "I feel better. I get dizzy and have headaches from time to time. Nothing to be upset about, possum."

He squeezed her hand. "That was quite a head bashing you took."

"What about you?"

"The leg is a bit gamy, but I get around."

Mary's expression changed to pensive. "Our mission to retrieve the scroll is out of the question after what happened."

David looked at the floor. "There's time for that discussion later. Put your energies into getting better and out of this bed."

Mary gave him a gentle nod of agreement. "What about Charles?"

He shifted his cane back and forth. "I'm not sure. I have tried to get information from the staff, but it's like pulling eye teeth. I believe he is in Dubai. They couldn't treat his injuries in Cairo. There was noise and fury with paperwork being signed. I only hope he is getting the medical help he needs."

Mary squeezed his hand. "You are a good man, David. I was right to pick you for this team. What has happened to us?"

"I'm not sure. The police questioned me after we arrived at the hospital, and told me it was a Muslim terrorist attack to stop the infiltration of American journalists."

"The equipment and Humvee are finished most likely."

"The Humvee has gone to meet its internal combustion maker. I caught a glimpse of the cameras and laptops and they were pretty beat up. The police impounded the lot, so I can't tell you if memory cards and hard drives can be recovered. No doubt we have to start from scratch once we get out of here."

***

Back at Langley, Scalisi's team worked at deciphering the Cairo intercept. Expecting to find nefarious activity relating to this collection of codified inscriptions, an even more puzzling revelation became clear.

The writing revealed another scroll existed, a thirteenth scroll. This scroll could lead to the exact location of Jeshua's remains. At first, Scalisi surmised it referred to the new leader of a jihadist cause, the spiritual leader of an important cell perhaps. After mulling his theory over a cup of cold coffee, he realized the writing referred to the lost scroll of Qumran.

The object intrigued him and he pursued further. Though he only had the photo file to work from, Scalisi kept Colby apprised of their progress, and along with his approval, he ordered a field team to Cairo at once. "Once again Colby's famous hunches bear worthy fruit," Scalisi thought.

He ordered a Lear jet to carry the team of four agents into Cairo. The next morning, they landed at the end of an airfield near Ciampino Airport and met with a military escort of two dark SUVs from the consulate already notified of their arrival.

Major Bruce Hammond met the team at the plane. Hammond, aware of the attack at the Berlin Hotel, believed it might be important. After a brief on the team's mission, he informed the team leader, Captain Jack Bannon, of the RPG incident. Bannon grunted with agreement. "Nice work, Hammond. It's a good place to start. Okay, we'll take it from here."

Hammond registered the rejection by Bannon, and yielded to his jurisdiction of the mission.

"Captain, we can provide intel and backup since we know the territory."

Bannon patted him on the shoulder. "Should occasion arise, we'll be in touch. See you later."

The captain leaned against an SUV and read the scroll translation while his team entered the hotel inquiring about the RPG incident. Cairo police had yet to clear the vehicle remains. Members of the team exited the hotel with little information to add to the investigation.

After reporting to Bannon, two team members interrogated the police officers sifting through debris in the front of the hotel and learned the victims had been sent to Cairo Medical Center. Half of the team went to the hospital to interview them as Bannon studied the translation and considered the location of the scroll. Though Bannon valued additional intelligence from the victims of the attack, he was more interested in the location noted in the translation.

The other two men joined him in the SUV. They arrived at the destination, a small storefront in the Khan el-Khalili Bazaar selling scarabs, eyes of Horus and anhk necklaces, postcards on wire racks, covered in a layer of forgotten dust. They entered the store half expecting to find a terrorist cell. An elderly Arab man sat behind a glass counter smoking a hookah with a young boy standing by idle. The man stared at the strangers carrying automatic weapons. He smiled, revealing crooked and missing teeth, and greeted them hoping they meant him and the boy no harm.

Bannon was charmed by the old man and looked through the dirty glass at the shelves of cheap pewter trinkets and necklaces. He wanted to confiscate a different booty. The boy cowered in the corner, shaking and frightened by the team's abrupt entrance. Bannon had limited Arabic linguistic skills; he returned the traditional greeting and demanded, "Where is the papyrus?"

The man let go of his hookah and threw up his hands declaring, "Alhamdulillah. I have no English. No English."

The boy feared for the elder's life and shouted in Arabic, "Why come here? My father can't help you. Don't hurt him. Don't shoot him."

Bannon directed his men to search the store. They tossed boxes, overturned chairs, and yanked the old man to the ground. He covered his face and yelled at his son, "Run boy, run."

After disheveling the store, they turned up nothing. Bannon yelled at the man to turn over the scroll.

The man curled on the floor and exclaimed, "I don't know what you talk about."

"Enough for English, liar? What else have you lied about?" said Bannon.

One team member in the back of the store continued throwing objects around to intimidate the storeowner. A torn tattered curtain revealed two crates covered in orange desert dust hiding an old wooden trap door.

"Sir, I may have found something."

Bannon rushed to the rear of the store as his team member pushed the crates aside. The trap door had not been opened in a long time. Its old rusted iron ring handle appeared unused. The team member tugged several times and then with one final pull, the door opened.

Down below, a dark hole widened into a cave.

The space descended eight feet below ground level. He shined his flashlight into the hole and realized he needed a rope to search further.

"Report, soldier. Tell me what we have," said Bannon.

The team member hesitated, and responded, "Can't tell sir. We need a rope to get down there."

"Check the SUV. Let's get to it."

Minutes later, the team member lowered himself below the floor. He landed and shined his flashlight around. "Sir, I see what looks like a barrel or an urn."

Bannon chuckled under his breath. "Check it out, we might get lucky."

The urn sat in a corner several feet from the entrance. A thick layer of dust on the floor caused the team member to walk slowly so as not to disturb more dust. He coughed twice.

"You okay down there, soldier?"

"I'm approaching the urn, sir."

The urn was three feet tall, fat in the middle rising to a tight neck at the top. It carried no markings and had a wooden lid for a cover. The team member removed the lid and peered inside with his flashlight. It was empty except for a terrible odor, like something rotten.

"Nothing here, sir. The urn is empty."

"Someone has beaten us to the prize. Come up, we're done here. Maybe the other team members have information at the hospital."

Bannon and his men headed for the Cairo Medical Center. Bannon hoped for results from the victims. The other half of his team stood in the corridor outside a ward and gave the captain their interrogation reports.

"Welcome, sir." The team member greeted Bannon with a salute. "We spoke to the woman and her colleague. They claim they knew about the scroll and its possible location, but never made because of the attack. They told us they were archeologists trying to locate the scroll for scientific purposes only."

Bannon put his hands against his waist with his fists clenched. He motioned for the team to regroup and return to their base of operations. Bannon had never failed before on a mission. He cursed the old man, Egypt, and his thickheaded team under his breath.

The Cairo Medical Center discharged Mary and she immediately sought out David. She entered his ward and found him sitting on his bed, dressed and ready with his belongings in a plastic bag by his feet.

"You ready to travel?" she said urgently.

David smiled. "Ready when you are, missy."

She looked at his bag, lamenting, "I assume the equipment has yet to be returned."

"Stuck at the Ministry of Interior. Leave it to Egyptians to embrace the worst forms of western bureaucracy."

"The gear can be replaced but what about Charles?"

"Perhaps Dr. Said will have more information. All I know is he was flown to Dubai and admitted him into a special clinic."

"We still need to find that scroll. First we'll ask about Charles, and then go over our notes to identify the scroll's location."

"As you wish, missy. Lead and I will follow."

Mary looked over her shoulder as she left the ward. "Replace that bag too. Makes you look like a refugee being repatriated."

Dr. Said gave Mary a reference number for Charles at the Ajman Specialty General Hospital outside of Dubai. She booked a flight that afternoon for her and David.

After takeoff from the Cairo International Airport, David turned to Mary in the airline seat next to the window. "I know Charles is important, but we must talk about the scroll, the notes you have that survived."

A half-filled cup of coffee had spilled on her tray table. The turbulence of the flight became more frequent; she ignored the coffee. "Charles is a good assistant, a bit more on occasion, and a decent man all around. The scroll will keep for a few more days. It's been buried for one thousand years where it is. I'm sure it's waiting for us."

"Many apologies for my selfishness. I mean no disrespect toward the boy."

"Accepted, possum."

Six hours later their plane landed with two bounces at Dubai International Airport.

"The pilot needs to practice his landing skills a little more," said David.

Mary chuckled. "What do you expect? He was likely trained at the same school the terrorists did for 9-11."

They hurried through the terminal to the taxi stand outside. Mary approached the lead taxi and asked the driver for his name.

"You are Americans, yes? I am called Mahmoud Amin."

"British really. We would like to go to the Ajman Specialty General Hospital."

Mohammed's brow wrinkled with concern. He threw up his hands and replied, "Ajman not in Dubai, in Ajman, maybe thirty miles from airport."

"Are you sure it's not in Dubai?"

"Sure as you are British. Drive taxi, pick up foreigners for twenty years, I know where things are. Give me any address and I find it. I say Ajman, it's in Ajman."

Mary slumped into the back seat with relief. "Yes, yes, you are correct. We'll enjoy the ride."

"What enjoy? Lots of desert, lots of people going other way to Dubai instead of Ajman."

On their arrival, the neon sign on the front of the modern building said "Ajman Specialty Hospital" in English and Arabic. Mary draped a scarf around her head before getting out of the taxi. She knew the local customs for women.

"You look positively Muslim, missy," said David.

"Try being a woman in this part of the world. The Arabs do not offer a lot of freedom for women."

The bland sand-colored hospital looked as though it had been disinfected on the outside. On past the main doors, floors shone bright with glistening marble and the ceilings were high enough to make a cold and distant echo. They approached the front desk hoping the receptionist behind the counter at a computer screen spoke their language.

She dressed in white with a matching burka covering her head, and spoke perfect English with only a slight accent.

"May I be of assistance?"

David prepared himself to speak, but Mary pushed forward usurping his attempt. "Why yes, thank you." She placed the note from Dr. Said on the counter. "I am looking for a patient admitted more than a month ago. He was British and injured in a grenade blast."

The receptionist reached for the telephone next to her computer. "Just a moment, please." She held a lengthy conversation in Arabic. "Take the elevators down that hall to the third floor and ask for Dr. Hajim."

David was disappointed that he didn't have time to apply his charm with the woman behind the counter. Mary detected his libido at work. "Settle down, possum. The time for romance is later, preferably back in England, and closer to your own age."

"I could have at least said hello, maybe asked for her cell phone number. Never been with a Muslim girl."

On the third floor, Mary and David noticed the

atmosphere was the same as hospitals elsewhere. Nurses shuttled to and fro a long corridor with determination while doctors stood in small groups discussing their cases. In the middle of the corridor was a high counter built with clipboards hanging along its edge. The height of the counter seemed to rise to the chest, leaving David to lean forward on his toes just to see over the top.

Every nurse wore a burka, making the hospital look like a nunnery. The doctors broke from their conversations long enough to notice Mary and David's presence, and turned back to ignore them.

Mary was too short to attract attention from the counter. She marched to a group of doctors and asked, "Does anyone know Dr. Hajim?"

One doctor asked in English rather gruffly, "What is your business?"

Mary replied in an equally curt manner. "We wish to speak with Dr. Hajim. He is treating a friend of ours."

"I see." He led them down the corridor. "Dr. Hajim's office is the second door on the right." Mary thanked him and headed for Hajim's office. David knocked on the open door and a voice spoke first in Arabic then in English. "Nem, tati fi fadlik. Yes, come in please."

Dr. Adnan Hajim looked up from behind his desk.

He sported a close-cropped beard and eyes framed by large black-rimmed glasses. The lenses were thick, showing his eyesight was poor. Mary determined he was small in stature but large in spirit. His medical jacket pocket, filled with pens, sported a stethoscope wedged between and dangled below. "Can I help you?"

"Thank you for seeing us," said Mary. "We are here to find out the status of our friend, Charles Osgood."

Dr. Hajim leaned back in his chair. He brought a pen to his mouth and pressed it against his lips before he spoke. "The British chap. Jolly good. Long Live the Queen." He ruffled through the papers on his desk for a ledger. He opened the pages revealing his schedule and stopped at the date of admission next to Charles's name.

"Here we are, yes. He came a month ago. Close to death when we received him. Not much of a chance to survive with his internal injuries. We have a fine facility with up-to-date equipment for analysis and treatment. We stopped the bleeding from his pancreas and saved his left kidney. He also had severe chest trauma, with one lung collapsed. Given his initial condition, he is doing much better. He is out of intensive care. You want to see him, yes?"

Mary was relieved and sighed. "Can we visit?"

"Why, yes. He is on the second-floor ward. I will take you."

"Thank you so much."

At the entrance to the ward, Dr. Hajim pointed to an area cordoned off by curtains. He said to Mary and David "You will find him inside."

Mary pulled back the curtains. Behind were two beds, one empty and the other filled with a man. Bandages covered his face.

David called out, "Osgood, friends have popped in for a visit."

The body did not move. Mary said, "Charles dear, it's us. David and I are here to see you."

Mary's heart dropped a beat and she feared the worst. "Charles, honey, can you hear me?"

Her mind raced over the doctor's words, wondering if she had misunderstood his description of her assistant's condition. She stepped close to the bed and placed her hand on the shoulder of the man, questioning whether he was Charles.

"Mary, is that you?"

She jumped back stunned at the voice coming from the bandages.

"Yes, it's Mary. I'm here with David to check on you."

Charles turned his head. "Bloody marvelous, it is you. I thought I was dreaming again."

Tears rolled down Mary's face. "Oh my, we are here for you. I'm so sorry we took so long to come. Can you see us, love? We are right near your bed."

Charles saw two shadows lit in a darkened space. "I can't. They keep me sedated me and I've been in a lonely dark fog most of the time."

"The doctor says you are recovering from your injuries. I thought you might be up and about."

Charles said with a weak chuckle, "No worries, just building a nice drug dependency I'll drown in Bass ale as soon as I'm home. I need more time is all."

"Do you remember what happened?"

"A bloody rocket hit the Humvee before I could undo my safety belt. Have you found the scroll?"

David put his arm around Mary's shoulder to comfort her.

"Not yet. We wanted to check on you before we made another attempt."

"You must find the damn thing, and without me. Science before sentiment is the rule, lady and gentleman. Now go out there and get it."

"We need you with us," said Mary.

"Don't worry your head about me. I'll be back before you can say 'Jack Robinson.' Besides, that ruffian you've been with is likely no fun. David, are you there?"

David rushed to answer. "I'm right here, thoughtless pup."

"You take care of our girl. Give me two weeks and I'll be out of this sand hill."

"We're counting on you."

"Don't drink up their gin," said Mary. "They might hold you for ransom."

Charles laughed a little. "Damn these Arabs. They don't have a drop to spare unless I break into the antiseptic cabinet to steal the rubbing alcohol."

They left the ward. David said to Mary in the elevator, "I wouldn't worry too much about Charles. He still has a fair amount of fight in him."

Despite his reassurance, worry over the health of Charles dominated her feelings as they left for the airport, her thoughts scrambled when she fumbled for a tissue. Despite her attempts to appear strong, tears fell like raindrops down her face.

Mary sat in the back of the taxi to the airport rolling through a mental fog accompanied by various street sounds that wove in and out of focus. David handled the tickets and boarding details. No sooner had they taken their seats than the plane's engines roared for takeoff. The drone put Mary into a deep sleep. David held her hand and stared out the window. The sun fell below the horizon and rain had come to Dubai. He watched the streaming water pass by, clouding his view of the ground breaking away. He longed to sleep and it eluded him.

His thoughts were a mishmash of images, codes danced like gremlins in his eyes and he doubted the worth of their mission. He worried about what other pitfalls lay ahead for the team. He stiffened with concern for Mary and Charles, and his mouth went dry.

A flight attendant approached and was ready to move past him when he tugged on her sleeve. "Excuse me, miss. Would you have gin handy on this flight?"

The attendant nodded yes and left him. She returned with a tray sporting a beautiful sight, a small glass of gin balanced in the middle of the tray, and gestured that he should take it. He smiled and tipped the glass in her direction to show his pleasure and gratitude. She left him to his drink.

The flight was long, six hours before they were back in Cairo. Mary slept and even the rough landing didn't interrupt her slumber. David hated to wake her, but the other passengers were deplaning and rushing by with hand-carried luggage slamming into them. He nudged her. "Wake up, missy. We're here."

Mary opened her eyes and was disoriented for a moment. She wiped at the saliva dripping from her mouth. A little embarrassed, she hoped no one had noticed. Passengers were in a hurry to get his or her baggage and deplane.

David stood with their bags in hand. Stepping into the aisle, she straightened her jacket to re-establish her poise. Smiling at David she said, "I slept right through. That's unusual for me as I'm always a little nervous flying."

"About three hours out we hit a patch of rough air. I was glad you slept through. You needed to rest your noggin, missy. Feeling better?"

"Let's get cracking. That scroll is in dire need of finding."

They checked in at the Oberoi Hotel without a hitch. The concierge recognized them and rang the bell for the bellman to take their luggage. "Come with me, we received your message and your rooms are set."

Mary was confused. David explained, "I took the liberty to call ahead, knowing you would want to freshen up when we arrived."

"Thanks, possum. You are turning thoughtful in your old age."

He had booked a suite with two bedrooms next to the lounge. It overlooked the Giza plateau basking in the morning sunlight. The bellman commented, "The rest of your luggage is arriving from the Berlin Hotel. If there is anything else you need, call me."

David pressed a few pounds into his hand. The bellman smiled and gave them a slight bow before leaving the room.

"Do whatever girlish things you must while I take advantage of the minibar begging to offer my fondest desire, which is bourbon. We can grab two hours sleep before we head out to the Khan el-Khalili Bazaar."

Mary called out from the bathroom. "I have had enough sleep for one day. Besides, I can't wait to get our hands on that bloody scroll."

"I anticipated your eagerness. I have a taxi ready to respond to our call."

"As you should. You know how I am about wasting time when there is work to do."

David prepared a double shot of bourbon on the rocks and Mary emerged from her bath dressed to travel. David gulped his bourbon.

"Waiting for an invitation?" She headed for the door. "Let's get going."

The taxi arrived in time to see the old man closing his shop for the day. Mary leaped from the taxi hailing him to stop in Arabic. "No, we must have a look in your store."

The man complained it was late, but he agreed when she promised to buy. He mentioned the men who had come before. "Americans," he said. Mary frowned. Her heart sank thinking they were too late.

"We're British and don't think much of them either. Too pushy for our tastes."

The old man laughed and said they left empty handed. He pulled back the curtain and pointed to the back. David led and Mary thanked the man for his kindness. The trap door had remained open from the previous attempt.

The storekeeper called for his son to bring a rope. He showed up moments later, handing David an old and shredded rope. He wondered if he could descend into the dark hole without breaking his legs, or get back out.

Mary secured the rope to a nearby post. With grunting and shifting his weight, David entered the hole and found the rope was short. He dropped the rest of the way, landing on his feet with a thud.

"I'll need a torch, Mary."

The old man passed Mary a battered flashlight and she tossed it down the hole.

"Here it comes."

"Damn, woman, you could have warned me."

"Sorry. You used to have fast hands."

"On the cricket pitch, missy. I see two urns but they are empty."

"Damn," Mary said under her breath.

David jumped for a hold on the rope, and fell back to

hit his head against the wall near the urns.

Mary called out. "What's that noise?"

"Just a small casualty." He picked himself off the floor and noticed a small hole where his head had slammed against the wall. "Wait a minute, I may have something."

David pulled at the edges of the hole. It was soft and broke in his hands. He tore an opening large enough to shine the flashlight inside. The wall was false, built for concealment.

The light flashed on another urn propped against the inside wall. David just reached the top of the urn with two fingertips. Tugging it, he tried to get a better hold. He made a desperate reach to grab the urn's upper lip.

"Bugger. Now I have you."

He dragged the urn toward him with several more tugs. The urn's mouth leaned to his grasp. He reached into the jar's mouth and felt the tip of a leather wrap. He smiled. After more fumbling, he pulled out a leather pouch.

"Mary, the scroll is ours. I'll toss it up to you, then try my best to get out."

"You are the best, possum."

After much tugging and pulling with Mary and the old man assisting, David emerged from the hole. He looked relieved.

Mary laid the scroll on the storekeeper's counter, eager to read the Aramaic, while David brushed the dust from his jacket and pants.

"Without the UV you won't see the marginalia," he said.

Mary's lip quivered as she scanned the writing. After several moments, her head lifted. Mary had gone pale with her eyes wide open. For a moment she could not speak. Then she found the composure to explain.

"They had no need to hide behind scrambled Farsi any more. Everything is out in the open and much bigger than we thought. According to this scroll, there is another one."

"Give it a rest, missy. This is getting to be like 'Dungeons and Dragons.'"

"Not at all. The other scroll reveals the tomb where they buried Jeshua's body."

"And that is close by, I trust."

"Not even. The Golan Heights."

Three black SUVs sped bumper-to-bumper, leaving a trail of dust longer than the vehicles put together. The dirt road led to a remote underground facility that carried a secret clearance requirement above cosmic level. Located deep in the Mojave Desert, certain covert operatives inside the NSA knew the facility as Site Y.

At the main gate of the compound, the SUVs stopped and the dust trail masked their presence temporarily after their arrival.

In the front SUV sat Silas Remy, CIA/NSA liaison for Special Operations, Alexander Colby, head of the CIA Directorate for Support, and Colonel Joshua Haig, SEAL team leader for Site Y. Sitting opposite them was Walter Harriman, Secretary of Defense, and beside him SEAL team officer, Colonel Briggs Stratton. The other SUVs held ten members of the SEAL support security team assigned to Site Y.

Above the ground, Site Y held little to look at. A single wood-frame building stood in the middle of a fenced area. The plaque hanging above its entrance read "United States Department of Environmental Research, Authorized Personnel Only." The double fence surrounding the building compound was ten feet high with rolled razor wire on top. Two soldiers toting automatic weapons patrolled the fence with attack dogs. An antenna dish mounted on the building's roof pointed at one of many military satellites orbiting above, and a small cell tower completed the installation.

The lead SUV came to a halt and the other two swerved to a sliding stop on each side. SEAL members piled out with automatic weapons at the ready and lined both sides of the entrance, following the same security protocol for the President.

Haig exited the lead vehicle and opened the door to allow Harriman, Colby, and Remy to exit. The three walked with determination toward the building, with Haig close behind. Once inside, an Air Force captain occupying a single desk asked for their security passes.

Behind the desk was a door leading to an inner storeroom. Once they had entered, Haig reached for the knife switch lever mounted on an adjacent wall. He pulled it down, creating a loud click and a low metallic hum. A metal wall emerged from both sides to close off the door. As the walls closed, the floor dropped to the levels below.

The elevator shaft took the group thirty floors below ground. When the elevator reached the last floor, another metal wall opened to reveal a thick glass door. Entrance through this door required voiceprint and retinal scan identification. SEAL team leader Haig provided these requirements and a computerized voice spoke. "Haig, Joshua, Colonel Marine, status, active. You're cleared to enter, Colonel."

The door opened with the hiss of a pressurized compartment. Haig turned to the others and explained. "A safeguard to prevent outside contaminates to enter the sensitive genetic and electronic facilities in the laboratory." The group nodded in recognition and approval.

Drs. Hubert Norvig and Heinrich Wolfram, top genetic biologists specializing in nanotechnology and artificial intelligence, welcomed the visitors.

"Greetings, gentlemen," said Norvig. "This is Special Project 2517. As you might imagine, we don't have many guests."

The room widened far and deep in a huge space illuminated with blue-white indirect light, and divided by an array of glass cubicles. Other scientists inside the cubicles were busy with separating genetic materials and recombining them. They watched the approaching strangers briefly before resuming their endeavors.

Other cubicles contained state-of-the-art computer control systems blinking with thousands of lights in random sequences and displaying complicated patterns. These provided monitoring and managed the entire operation.

In the largest space was a glass-enclosed room, where a large cylinder hung above a gray pedestal by two large metallic rings at each end, connected to the ceiling by thick metal cables. Lined on both sides with dials, the pedestal held gauges and colored buttons lighted to reflect the conditions in the cylinder.

At each end, the pedestal connected to the cylinder by hundreds of cables and pipes. The cylinder was filled with a milky clear liquid more viscous than water. Small streams of bubbles trailed from the bottom of the cylinder and dissolved before they reached the top. The cylinder, illuminated by the surrounding blue-white light, was the focal point of the facility.

Suspended in the cylinder was a large nude human body. It floated in the fluid and the extremities twitched from time to time, showing there was life present.

The group passed hundreds of glass cylinders that lined both sides of the main aisle. Inside each cylinder were anatomical forms in various stages of mutation. Many revealed a startling presentation of awe and horror, representing genetic success and failure.

Norvig and Wolfram flanked the group as they

proceeded through the hideous display of Frankenstein-like experiments, which provided a narrative of the facility and commented on the various developmental stages.

Their path led to the large horizontal cylinder room. This represented the pinnacle of their achievement.

"Gentlemen, what you see before you represent two years of intense genetic development," Norvig said. "Project 2517 is the development of an advanced super soldier/being, made for the military at considerable expense."

Harriman pointed at the cylinder. "It's moving. Is it alive?"

"Well yes. The hybrid construct of genetic engineering is aided by nanotechnology," Wolfram said. "Though the specimen is moving, it only means the nanites, micro-miniature electronic devices in the body, are regulating the internal organic functions, much like you would expect in a sophisticated machine."

"It's a robot," said Harriman.

Norvig jumped in. "Much more than a robot, it's the perfect combination of simulated organic tissue and artificial intelligence. The structures include a localized program that controls their actions. However, when synchronized, the nanites function as one mind, working together as a colony. This kind of arrangement you would find with a typical hive mentality."

"Is it conscious?" asked Harriman.

"Not yet," said Wolfram. "The nanites function as a subroutine localized to a master program that provides the overriding awareness and system control. At the moment, the specimen is in a suspended state, much like a human in a coma. The superior functions of strength, agility, and speed occur by virtue of the AI immune system, created by the combined efforts of the nanite colony. When the body is damaged, its repair occurs instantly. This makes the body almost invincible to wounds or attack."

"You mentioned that these 'nano' things are a subroutine," said Colby. "What or where is the master program that makes it work?"

"To be honest, we haven't affected an AI program adequate to manage the nanites," Norvig answered. "The colony subroutine resists another program interfering with their functions. They want to operate as a closed system. We're thinking of another approach. The nanites need a higher functioning control system they will yield to. We are simulating an external artificial mind, or 'over-soul' for the creature to function as a liaison with the nanites."

Remy joined in. "If you succeed, would the creature be obedient and respond to commands without question? Will it follow any orders?"

Norvig looked at Remy with disapproval. "Of course, and without moral convictions. The goal is killing the enemy without remorse."

"It will be a perfect soldier or agent?" asked Harriman. Norvig nodded in the affirmative. "We waited five years for the Predator drone to come on line. That was a simple AI fix, they said. What can we expect with this project? Congress is itchy to pull the plug on these fringe covert programs that don't show results."

"Don't worry, Mr. Secretary," said Wolfram. "We are close, but we need a little more time, that's all." "You had better show serious progress or heads will roll and mine will not be one of them. If you get my drift, gentlemen." Harrington turned to Colonel Haig. "I have seen enough. Now get me back upstairs. Don't you agree?" He glanced at Colby and Remy, and they nodded in agreement.

As soon as the elevator started its long climb to the surface, Wolfram turned to Norvig. "You lied. We don't have the answer yet, you idiot. We are not even close."

Norvig placed his hand on Wolfram's shoulder. "You worry too much. We'll come up with something soon."

"This is your department. You had better be right."

"You always freak out at the slightest sign of difficulty, my friend. I thrive on this shit."

Mary and David arrived at the Museo Egizio in Rome late in the evening. After unlocking the door to the scroll room and turning on the light, the room remained silent and vacant. Mary realized the missing piece was Charles. She found it difficult being there with his absence.

Like a tear in a favorite garment, not having him there to share in their triumph was unfair. Her depression set in and David picked up on her lament. He went straight for the bourbon bottle sitting on the card table where they left it.

She dropped into her chair looking dejected. He held up a paper cup checking for any stain before making an offer. "Brighten up, missy. I know you miss him, but don't worry. He'll be back soon and complaining he missed the fun and the bourbon." He looked into her saddened eyes. "You could use a drink." David filled the cup and extended it to her. "I hate to drink alone, even when I do."

Mary scowled. "It's too late in the evening."

David made a sad clown face. "Or too early for late risers."

"All right, but just a small one. Alcohol keeps me up and we have a heavy day tomorrow."

"It's just a nightcap, a nerve tonic for restless spirits."

Mary chuckled. "In our work, spirits are always

restless and ancient."

The next scroll had a problem with location. The Golan Heights was a troubled area for Israel, marked by constant skirmishes with the Palestinians over settlements. Getting permission to enter would be difficult, especially if the Israeli government knew their purpose was to find an ancient relic. Israel took a dim view of any outside party going after relics on their land.

Mary knew it would require serious effort to get permission and an agreed-upon joint effort. She had to call in favors.

David woke on the couch in the reception area with a stiff neck. He looked around to find Mary. David called her name toward the other offices until he heard her behind him.

"I'm behind the scroll room on the phone."

Mary slumped over a low table with a telephone receiver to her ear.

"The landlines in Rome are uncommonly wretched. I've been on this phone for an hour before I had any contact."

Mary heard a faint female voice say, "We have your connection, please hold."

She gritted her teeth, and her eyes seemed to draw inward, focus realized with fierceness.

The voice returning was male. "Mary, what are

you doing in Rome, dancing in the Trevi fountain?
It's Howard, waiting at your beck and call. It's been
too damn long."

"Memories do not fade with time. I need help
with a bit of red tape."

Howard Cooper had functioned as chief White
House correspondent for The Washington Post
before hooking up with a very wealthy lobbyist.
Through several favors owed the lobbyist, he
became Chief of Staff to the President.

He was a fantastic contact for Mary. She needed
approval from the State Department and Howard
knew the Secretary of State from golfing at the same
club.

Mary asked how much Howard remembered
being in London on assignment. He left out the
promise to uphold an owed favor owed.

"Listen, Howard, you will not weasel out of this
one. I won't let you. I have a little leverage on my
own."

"You're a British subject who wants the U.S.
State Department assistance in getting you into
somewhere you're not supposed to be. Is that all?"

"Actually two British subjects, and we want to go
to the Golan Heights for a matter of utmost
archeological importance. We need documents from
the State Department signed by the Secretary

himself, and visas to Israel and an introductory letter addressed to the head of Shabak, the Israel Security Agency."

"Go pick on your own government. Do you want my liver and spleen too?"

"My government would tell me to go spin, or wait, or spin and wait. Besides, your government gives more money to the Israelis than we do. By the by, the last time I checked my liver and spleen were fine."

She hung up and turned to David with disgust. "I hate politicians. I always feel in need of a thorough scrubbing when I've shaken hands with one."

"Stop expecting them to be honest. Can he help us?"

"Of course he will, silly old bastard. This happened before he met his current inamorata, but Howard chased around London after a tart who worked as a hostess in a private gentleman's club when he was supposed to be writing about how we were helping the Yanks track down bin Laden. I had been asked to help him with the geography of the search area by the British Museum, and ended up helping him avoid arrest when she accused him of stalking. The girl in question was actually quite nice and had taken a first in Elizabethan poetry."

David cocked his head. "Missy, sometimes you

scare the hell out of me."

"You don't know the half of it, possum. I've been around and survived many skirmishes and still walked away with my scalp. One such situation brought me to my elegant position as head of conservation. You see, my dear possum, a woman must know her resources and be able to use them when needed."

David felt as though he were present at a military staff meeting. He had thought of Mary as head strong, but her prowess at tactical manipulation was a shock.

Hours later, a courier arrived at the reception desk asking for Mary's signature to release the package he carried. She returned to David in the scroll room.

"They are here. Let's see what Howard drummed up."

She tore the envelope open and dumped the documents at the end of the scroll table. They stood in awe of what lay before them, every document and credential Mary had asked for.

She turned to David. "Book a flight for Tel Aviv. We are on our way, possum."

By morning, they landed at the Ben Gurion International airport. As their plane approached Terminal 3, an armored vehicle pulled close to the ramp. Passengers disembarked, with Mary and

David not far behind. Three officers from the Israeli Security Agency pulled them from line and ushered them into the vehicle.

Mary pulled out the State Department documents, exclaiming, "We have approval from your government." The officers ignored her and Mary stayed silent for the rest of the journey.

Shabak headquarters was located between the Ayalon freeway and the bus terminal. Tourists and hikers were regularly warned about getting too close to the building. The officers got out and pulled Mary and David from the back, keeping a firm grip on them into the cold building of the Israeli Security Agency, also known as Shin Bet, whose motto was "The Unseen Shield."

They were ushered into a small office and told to sit down. The room was plain, smelling of desert and cigar smoke. A portrait of Prime Minister Benjamin Netanyahu hung above the empty desk with two chairs positioned in front. They sat down, waiting for something to happen.

Moments later, the door opened to a stout husky man dressed in a well-pressed military uniform. He entered without saying a word. His uniform was gray compared to the officer in blue standing by the door, and carried a side arm covered by a leather flap at his waist. He walked behind the desk holding a thick folder, dropped the folder on the desk and sat down. At first, he opened the folder with surprise, followed by noticeable disapproval. Perusing the contents of the folder was a useful distraction.

The officer looked at Mary and David with piercing gray blue eyes. He had a mustache that hung over a half-smoked cigar protruding from the side of his mouth. He shifted the cigar from one side to the other before he spoke.

"You have come before me with enough documents to paper these walls. But why, I ask myself, are these people here? It has already begun, you see. My day begins with suspicion and trouble. My nose tells me you are at the heart of it."

Mary risked an additional charge of insolence. "Who might you be, may I ask?"

He glared at her. "Miss Russo, I am Lieutenant General Moshe Cohen, head of Shin Bet. You seem to have a great deal of influence with the American government. I am not in the habit of being summoned to cater to anyone's antics, and yours is no exception. They asked me to cooperate in any way I can on your behalf. But this is the State of Israel and I am the law. What happens in this country does not pass my desk without my permission."

"I'm sorry for troubling you, General Cohen. I only wanted to ensure that we had proper permission before proceeding with our search."

The general leaned back in his chair. "And what are you searching for?"

Mary hesitated, trying hard not to lose her composure. "My colleague and I are here in search of a relic, a document with important historical and archeological significance. We examined the scrolls from Nag Hammadi and came across new evidence of other scrolls."

"Why come to us? These are history, what has this got to do with Israel?"

"This may be the key to discovering the greatest archeological find of the century. We believe, General, you should be a part of this find."

The general softened. He reached into the desk and pulled open a drawer on the right side. Out came a bottle of whiskey. He sat it on the desk and looked to the officer standing nearby.

"Why are you standing there? Bring glasses for our guests."

The officer turned and left the room. "Please excuse the slow hospitality. Officers have no experience with proper protocol. Miss Russo, tell me more about this relic of yours."

Mary explained their discovery of the ancient Farsi writing on the Qumran scrolls and how this led them to the thirteenth scroll in Cairo, which led them to another scroll in the Golan Heights, and brought them to Israel.

General Cohen said, "The Heights were excavated and developed. Nothing of what you speak was found."

The officer arrived with the glasses. He placed them on the desk and returned to his original stance by the door at the ready.

The general smiled while pouring the whiskey. He handed one glass to Mary and then David, who sighed when the glass touched his lips. General Cohen lifted his glass and pointed to them.

At three o'clock on Friday afternoon on a Friday, Alexander Colby tidied his desk. He moved files from the top of his desk into a drawer out of sight. It was how he put that day's issues to bed, for a short time. Other issues and other files on Monday would meet a clean slate, the surface of his desk devoid of old litter.

Colby was a good director. Even though he had occasion to order indecent things done, his heart was in the right place. He would not hesitate to help a fellow case officer or mitigate an internal conflict to achieve justice for all concerned. He was fastidious and neat to a fault. Colby was a quiet man, yet wasn't above chastising an officer for improper attire. He held up well under pressure and believed himself to be a true patriot.

On Fridays, he planned for escape to his houseboat on Chesapeake Bay. It almost never worked out in his favor. Something always turned up at the last moment, a problem that didn't sit well with Mrs. Colby.

Colby closed his briefcase and reached for his coat when his hopes faded as he watched Remy headed for his office. Colby looked down at his watch thinking, if he left now, he would just make the ferry. His gaze shifted back at Remy and there it was, that unmistakable look of determination. He thought, if Remy was that determined at three minutes to six o'clock then it was serious, but if not, he would have Silas working weekends until his retirement. Colby smiled, hoping at that moment it was the case.

Remy entered Colby's office and closed the door behind him. Colby maneuvered into his chair behind his desk.

"What's on your mind this late in the day?" He scowled.

"You remember the code anomaly we stumbled across out of Egypt last week? I kept trying to break the code using a well-known Sumerian cypher for three days without success, until last night. I cross-referenced the code with NOVA, our latest AI data bank, and an obscure paper by Dr. David Cross, a respected archeologist and cypher analyst of several esoteric codices. Using his cypher allowed me to break the code twenty minutes ago."

Colby was only half listening. Every word out of Remy's mouth pushed back further his fantasy weekend. It slipped away with every passing moment. In a flash of fury and rage, he shouted at Remy. "My God man, get to the point!"

"It wasn't a terrorist plot after all, that attack on the archeologist's Humvee."

"Your task is to find the bad guys that make plans

to blow us to hell. This is outside your purview."

"Yes sir, that's right."

Colby pounded on his desk. "If the attack wasn't done by terrorists, then why are you taking up space and sucking up the air in my office?"

"You are the most pigheaded man I have ever laid eyes on. That said, I'm trying to tell you the message is much more significant. I have learned what is on that scroll. It could be very important to us and significant for our interests."

Colby tried to be civil and mindful of his rising blood pressure. "What does the scroll have, a new and improved recipe for hummus?"

"The message came from the laptop man in Cairo, not from him just through him. It says there is another scroll that reveals the location where Jeshua's body is buried."

Colby looked at Remy as though time had stopped. The silence in the room was deafening. If the actual body of Jeshua was recovered, who knew what might happen? The power he wielded on Earth would be present as if he was alive. The thought staggered Colby's imagination.

He had to admit that Remy's news might end their desperation for a breakthrough on Project 2517. Colby imagined the successful conclusion of the project and of receiving honors for creating a perfect soldier or ideal diplomat.

"Remy, we've had our differences in the past and if this turns out to be true, I will extend to you my heartfelt apology. I also have to admire your tenacity in this matter. Do you think it's possible some of his power lies dormant with his interred bones? Perhaps we can explore taking advantage of this opportunity. We need to make this happen."

Colby picked up the telephone and called Secretary of Defense Walter Harriman. He requested a secure line and told Harriman of their discovery. Colby went on about how they should expedite a team to find the second scroll, recover the artifact, and ship it to Site Y.

He said, "Israel must realize the mission's importance, that it is a matter of extreme national security and considered classified." Harriman agreed. He called Norvig and Wolfram and informed them of the new developments. Then he placed a call to Israel and his good friend, Lieutenant General Cohen.

"Perhaps we can be of service." He downed the shot in a single swallow. "My whiskey is not the best, but it does cut the dust from the palate. Now, tell me about this Farsi code of yours."

General Cohen insisted that Mary and David try accommodations in the old port of Jaffa. "I have taken the liberty to put you in the Setai, right along the Mediterranean Sea. You will find the stay comfortable while we arrange your expedition."

Mary was stunned by the sudden shift in the general's attitude. She turned to David, who shrugged his shoulders. "I'm not particular about where I sleep. I'm fine with any shelter that keeps the dust out and the rain off my head. If a hot bath, decent bourbon, and good food are included, so much the better."

"Thank you, General, for your hospitality on such short notice," said Mary. "Until tomorrow?"

Cohen nodded. "Yes, tomorrow."

The thirty-minute taxi ride to the hotel from the Shabak headquarters followed the shoreline. David remarked to Mary as the driver pulled into circular entrance of what was once a jailhouse during the Ottoman Empire, "Wow. He was right about comfortable. Setai is posh in the right places."

Their rooms were next to each other, connected by separate doors to the bathroom. David opened his side and looked into Mary's room. This presented an interesting dilemma.

"Timing needs negotiating," he said.

Mary allowed the lid of her suitcase to drop. "I

want to take a long soak right now. Do you have a problem with that? I promise to leave enough hot water for a shave."

"My concern is with my belly and brains being about two liters shy of good whiskey. I'll be going to the bar, missy."

Mary sat on the edge of the bed and brushed her hair. She stared at the tub and the steam coming off the water while thoughts of Cohen's conversation spun in her head, leaving an uneasy feeling in her stomach.

She stuck her head around David's door. "I have a terrible presentment about the dear general. Our hats were handed to us, so to speak, and the general is only playing at having our best interests at heart. I bet he is working to gain the advantage at this moment."

"Let's say you are right. What should we do?"

"Get your travel boots, possum. We go scroll hunting."

"Calm down, missy. We can be foolish tomorrow just as well as today. Let's call this a vacation day. All work and no play make Jack and Jacqueline very dull indeed."

***

Cohen turned the key to lock his office door and the phone on his desk rang. He wanted to ignore the call, but his better judgment told him to answer.

He picked up the receiver to hear an unfamiliar voice. "This is President Yitzhak Herzog, calling from the office of the prime minister. Am I speaking with General Moshe Cohen?"

"Yes, your Excellency."

"General, I have received a call from the President of the United States with a special request made by the Secretary of Defense, that you must detain Mary Russo and her associate, David Cross. They have stolen documents from the Museum of Egyptian Antiquities in Cairo and are wanted for questioning. They are trying to claim certain artifacts that, if their recovery efforts become public before the situation can be managed, may prove deleterious to our mutual political and economic concerns and futures. The Americans are sending a special team to extract and secure the artifacts from the wrong hands, as agreed by both governments at the highest levels."

Cohen sighed. A cloud of disappointment moved across his face. This wild gambit might have worked, maybe even been profitable, he thought. Now it will fall out of his control and into the hands of the upper echelons of power.

"Yes, your Excellency, I understand. If Russo and Cross are in search of artifacts, would it not be more prudent to put them under surveillance until tomorrow morning? They might contact confederates, and we would like to know anyone working with them."

"Such a stratagem might be helpful. Very well, act with the utmost discretion. We are counting on you, General Cohen. It's imperative these people fail in their attempts to steal more documents."

"Yes, your Excellency, no problem. Thank you, your Excellency."

He hung up the phone.

***

David rose early as a matter of habit from so many digs in his career. He called room service and ordered breakfast with coffee delivered to Mary's room, along with a note: "Hope you are hungry. May I join you?"

Wearing a robe over pajamas, Mary opened the door to a linen-draped cart rolled in laden with a cornucopia of breakfast delights, with David behind the small parade of hotel staff.

"What is this about?" Mary chided.

"I thought that after a difficult night of bathing

and languid sleeping you would be voracious. You are, aren't you?"

Mary gazed at the selections on the cart, which softened her attitude. "You are beyond exasperating sometimes, but nice to have around. Come in. Besides, I hate to eat alone."

Once the staff left them, Mary and David talked about Charles, their successes and failures with the scrolls, and the strength of Israeli coffee. Mary expressed her concerns about their current situation. She had no trust in the general and lamented there was little they could do if his support was not forthcoming.

"Cohen seems like an all-right sport," countered David. "Besides, I recognized the signs of greed and avarice gleaming from his eyes. I bet he will play along because he has everything to gain and nothing to lose."

***

When they confirmed the missing scroll, Colby wasted no time in scrambling a team. He directed the traffic staff to contact field operatives in the vicinity of Riyadh. Two helicopters assigned to the CIA team waited on the helipad for their arrival. The team drove from the western gate of Al-Madhbah into

Riyadh and learned of their mission when they were in flight.

Colonel Herbert Straker spoke to the men aboard his helicopter and addressed the men in the second by radio. The rotor noise was loud inside the cabin although they were flying in whisper mode. The colonel raised his voice over the noise.

"Men, this mission is unusual as it may not fall into the category of a firefight, but I want you to stay frosty just in case anything goes wrong. The purpose is extraction, but not in the sense you may think. We are searching for a missing artifact in hostile territory, which may lead to an extraction. This is a national security issue and considered classified." Major Elliot "Hap" Stone, Straker's second in command, asked, "What is it we are looking for, Colonel?"

Straker looked at him with the respect of brothers-in-arms, having fought together for two tours in Iraq and one in Afghanistan before signing with the Agency. He felt good knowing Stone was with him. Stone was called Hap because he always had a smile on his face, even under fire.

"A scroll made of parchment or papyrus that will lead us to another scroll and then recovery and extraction of an important object. The scrolls describe the location of the object. One leads to another."

Captain Cecil Armstrong leaned around the troops to ask Colonel Straker where they were going.

"Our coordinates are for caves in the Syrian-held side of the Golan. The mission goes tonight and we could draw attention and be fired on by Syrian rebels in the area. The coordinates are also right in the middle of a no-fly zone.

"We should arrive in about four hours. Once we set down, I want three men inside the cave and the rest to fan out and create a perimeter around the entrance. In a surprise attack, those outside the cave will use the Delta assault pattern. Is everybody clear?"

The men in his helicopter shouted, "Sir, yes sir" in unison. Straker listened for a similar response over the radio. The volume was low and a little tinny, but he smiled on hearing an echo of acknowledgement.

The helicopters landed, and Straker and Stone jumped out to survey the situation. They gave the high sign that all was clear. Field operatives followed with bags and bundles of equipment and weapons. Every man hurried and hauled their hardware and weapons into position, while the team assigned to the cave carried their bags to the entrance.

***

Mary called the concierge for a taxi while David started carrying their bags down the winding staircase. He spotted officers from the Israeli Security Agency at the hotel entrance, and realized Mary had been more accurate than he surmised and ran back up the staircase.

"You are going in the wrong direction, missy."

"David, what's happening?"

He grabbed her arm and ushered her along the upper promenade. "Cohen gave us up to someone we don't want to be given up to and his hardy men are waiting for us. We can't use the main entrance. Most likely we'll be restrained here or at their headquarters."

They rounded the back of the promenade that led to an exit.

"I have an idea," said Mary. "We'll walk to Beit Eshel and call for a taxi from Market House. It's a trendy boutique hotel that costs too much. We'll blend with the locals while we wait. I never thought reading magazines in the bath would come in helpful."

She called the taxi company with her cell phone and made a peculiar request. "Could you have the driver pull up in front of the Setai and wait for five minutes before you pick us up at the Market House?"

"Gladly, madam," said the dispatcher. "Should the driver expect a passenger from the Setai to join you?"

"We have friends staying there and they want to know when we are leaving."

"An excellent precaution. The car will be at the Setai in fifteen minutes, then at Market House five minutes later."

"Thank you. That will be fine."

Mary turned to David. "How do we get across the street without being seen?"

David pulled Mary along the staircase descending in back of the promenade. They started down the staircase half running when Mary broke the heel on one of her shoes. She hopped without missing a step and removed the other shoe and kept running. They were soon on the street and had to cross an open square. David spotted a bus approaching the stop on a nearby cross street.

"Stick with me, brave missy. We'll walk down the street to the bus stop, get on the bus, and when it pulls up to the first stop beyond Market House, we'll get off and walk back without being discovered."

Mary was nervous about David's plan of escape, but was at a loss to think of anything else. She followed his lead.

David hailed the bus and they settled into seats until the bus stopped as soon as it started. The Israeli Security Agency interrupted any further travel.

Officers walked around the bus and beckoned the driver to open the doors. Mary buried her face in her hands. "We're going to an Israeli prison."

The driver argued with the ISA officers about traffic and impossible schedules, and the bus went on. Mary and David signaled the driver they wanted out at the next stop. He shrugged his shoulders and nodded, causing the half-smoked cigarette hanging from his lips to drop ash on his knee. He brushed it away and stepped on the gas. Soon they were off the bus and walked to the Market House.

As he and Mary ascended the steps of the hotel, a policeman asked David, "Have any American smokes on you?" David stuck out open hands and the police waved him on. He let out a silent sigh. His plan had worked. They watched from the Market House as their taxi arrived in front of the Setai.

The ISA officers questioned the driver, and he told them he was waiting for a couple to take them into the city. The officers waved him on and he swung around to pull up in front of the Market House. Mary and David jumped in.

Mary asked the driver his name.

"Hassam at your service, Israeli father and Palestinian mother, I have no opinions on politics or religion. Where you go, I take you, and at reasonable rates.

"We want to go to the Golan Heights."
He said, "The Golan is too rough. Syria still holds the eastern part. Such a trip will cost you plenty."

"We don't care how much it costs, and we also want you to stay and wait for us."

Hassam balked. "Madam, I want to help you but I have children to feed. This is too dangerous for a family man."

Mary pulled several bills from her purse. "Will one thousand American dollars help change your mind?"

Hassam squirmed in his seat. "One thousand dollars you say?"

Mary showed him the ten $100 bills clutched in her hand.

"Agreed, and I want an extra $200 for waiting."

"You drive a hard bargain. Let's go."

"Where you want is desolate, nothing is there, I assure you."

"We want to see the caves."

"Limestone, water, not many caves. It would be safer for all of us if you visited the museum in Tel Aviv."

"What we are looking for isn't in a museum, at least not yet."

The heat from the morning sun increased during the two-hour drive to the caves. David rolled down his window. Dust rising from the road, he felt, was more tolerable than the heat pouring from the engine into the taxi. Hassam apologized to David for his air conditioner that failed two days before. He hadn't had time to get it fixed.

When the taxi neared the caves, Mary wanted to hold back. She told Hassam to stop before the next turn off and park near the trees.

Mary and David left him and walked the hill toward the turn off. The view opened at the top of the hill and they looked at a military spectacle.

Desert-camouflage Humvees blocked every direction. Troops setting up their perimeter took no notice of the onlookers. Mary said, "We're too late. Someone high up already knows what's at stake."

"Any ideas about alternatives? My vote is to turn back," said David.

She gritted her teeth. "I'm not giving up, not now, never. We have to get into the cave."

David looked at the armed troops gathering into a defensive camp.

"We have crossed the Rubicon and met our match. We don't have weapons. Do you expect to get in there with an innocent smile?"

"I know, I know. I'm trying to think and you're not helping."

"Sorry, missy. It's unrealistic to consider taking on the authorities."

"General Cohen sold us to the highest bidder and judging from the looks of things, it looks like the CIA won."

Just as Mary was about to march into the camp, Syrian rebels fired an RPG that sailed over her head to destroy a Humvee and kill three soldiers.

Mary saw her opportunity—use the chaos in the camp as a distraction, sneak in and grab the scroll, and escape while the others continued to fight.

David worried they would end up under a burning Humvee during the assault. Mary stiffened and insisted they act now while the battle raged.

They crept between burning vehicles, large boulders, and dead soldiers from both sides, dodging automatic gunfire with explosions sprouting like mushrooms in the dust. Soldiers were so involved in the firefight they paid no attention to the maneuvers of the intruders.

The mouth of the cave was dark and large enough to enter without a squeeze. Once inside, the space opened into a wider expanse. The cave floor inclined toward a ceiling dripping with stalactites that had to be crouched under as they entered.

Mary scanned for signs of old urns that might hold the scroll's location. David picked through the sand and dust for any objects they could use.

"David, come here for a moment."

"What have you found?"

Mary pointed to scrape marks in the sand and dust on the floor of the cave from something being dragged. They followed the marks to an anteroom, and a large urn on its side with its wood cover torn off, plundered and empty.

The gunfire ceased and the pair waited in the cave until it was safe to make an escape. Mary and David peered over the boulders resting nearby. Carnage spread in every direction, and no sign of the rebels. She turned to David. "Check their clothing and look for anything that resembles a leather pouch."

"This entire escapade has made you bloodless. These are human beings."

"Dead human beings, and they can still be useful. Now shut up and get to work."

Several minutes passed as Mary and David searched for the scroll. Mary slouched on the torn fender of an overturned Humvee and David stood up with a leather pouch clutched in his hand.

"Look what we have here."

Mary rushed over and seized it. She unwrapped

the covering and found a partial piece of the original parchment. In their rush to defend the camp from the Syrian rebels, the CIA field operatives didn't realize the parchment came as two parts. They had the first but the second was left behind.

Mary found a flashlight and flicked it on. Scanning the parchment revealed small writing in ancient Farsi. The miniscule writing made identifying the words difficult.

David used a magnifying glass for closer study. His mouth fell open and he turned to Mary.

"This refers to location of Jeshua. The CIA is looking for his body, Mary."

She lowered her head. Why would the government be interested in the body of Christ? This could be the greatest archeological find of the last millennia.

David studied the characters, puzzled by their arrangement. They were duplicated and put in backwards to face each other. David had seen this technique used in a dig near the Sudan, where an ancient puzzle cloaked the hiding place of one of the most sought-after mummies in recent history. Mary was distraught over losing the first part of the scroll. David was hopeful. He thought he could isolate the characters to duplicate the first part, directions to the location. The impact of such a find would be catastrophic to the spiritual and religious life of millions of followers of Christianity.

The hour was late. Neither David nor Mary would stop from a little fatigue. They worked at a fever pitch until their efforts paid off. They knew scroll would lead them to the burial place of Jeshua.

The early morning light of the sun cast shadows over the desert landscape near Site Y. The sunlight's reflection glimmered, dancing from the windshield of the lead SUV to the next, moving close behind while in the rear a Humvee gathered dust from another vehicle's wake. The cloud of dust rolled past them with greater momentum as the vehicles came to a halt at the gate of Site Y.

Four soldiers from the lead SUV positioned themselves to receive the cargo inside the second SUV. They opened the side doors and rear hatch to bring the container in reach and remove it from the vehicle.

The pressurized container represented the latest biological preservation unit. It isolated its occupant from any outside contagion. The unit also functioned in the opposite direction, to protect the environment from contagion held in the container.

Despite burial for two thousand years, the remains were in a preserved state. The soldiers had survived the attack in the Golan Heights, Major Stone having lost Colonel Straker to Syrian gunfire. They were very careful handling the fragile bones, containing traces of marrow holding the DNA that Site Y wanted, and hurried to bring in the body.

Knowing what lay before them on the examination table created palpable silence from those present. The awe of what they had brought back from the Golan was in everyone's mind, but no one wanted to speak of it, an unconscious reverence for what might be physical evidence of God on earth. Dr. Norbert broke the silence.

"All right people, let's move with a purpose."

He directed the soldiers to set the case down next to the gurney and examined the digital readouts of the container's environmental control system. The container was intact. Site Y's computer took over recycling the air and establishing positive pressurization. A loud burst from a klaxon horn confirmed the change and the flashing red light changed to a steady green. The remains were then removed from the container.

When the seal broke, the overhead lights dimmed and the secondary UV came on. This startled Benjamin Soames, the young engineer standing by. The man next to him said, "The interface of the container matches the computer interface, so we connected the case to the central computer before it was opened. The central computer sensed a seal break and flooded the room with ultraviolet light as protection for us. Nothing to worry about, there aren't any supernatural forces at work."

Jeshua was smaller than expected. His body was wrapped and skin tissue stretched over the bones like leather. The body was well preserved given the centuries it was at the mercy of the elements. The hair was dark, woven with a swipe of gray, and had continued to grow beyond his demise, reaching almost to the hip. The eye sockets were concave, but the eyes were more present than expected.

Norvig stood in a small huddle questioning where to extract DNA material when the corpse has been dead for two thousand years. He knew what bone he would take the extraction from before he posited the question, which he had stated only for thoroughness.

"Gentlemen, I believe we should start here." He pointed to the upper portion of the patella leading to the lower portion of the femur bone.

"If we make a linear incision along the ridge, we can extract several lines of petrified marrow for our purposes."

The other scientists present gave a nod or grunt of approval.

Hours later, Jeshua's core femur material was sectioned and isolated through an inertial centrifuge, then separated magnetically. The scientists looked at the genetic material for an active state with the electron microscope. They took several samples that showed signs of awakening in vitro with pulsed high frequency energy. The process of reanimation was Dr. Wolfram's area of expertise, having won the

Nobel Prize for advanced biology and chromosome research.

After two days of sequencing and pairing, success came in the extraction and awakening. They formulated a serum from the awakened samples and introduced the serum to the passive body in the cylinder. A large syringe on the order of a hypodermic injection glowed with faint phosphorescent rose-colored golden hue.

The team took care to administer the serum outside the cylinder by remote. If a violent reaction occurred, maintaining control was a priority. The scientists held their collective breath as they expected their creation.

At first, no reaction was present, except for the body twitching at the beginning of injection. The group stood in front of the cylinder and considered other options. Then the body shuddered from head to toe. Norvig ordered a halt to the injection. Jeshua's DNA had met with great resistance from the nanites. After many cups of cold black coffee, Wolfram turned to Norvig and said, "Look at the sequences under the microscope and our little friends are trying to decode his DNA backwards. That tells me to reverse the polarity of the peptides in the chromosomes and then the transmission should work."

Norvig shouted, "Get to it, people. The week is still young."

For a moment, engineers and scientists looked at each other. As if a shot was fired to start a foot race, they broke up and scurried to their cubicles to begin the re-sequencing and polarization of the chromosomes.

Five days later, the round-the-clock effort had left many sleeping bodies in various places around the lab. Norvig, awake with his head propped up by his left elbow, glanced at his watch.

"It's been over three hours since the last separation. Let's see if the cycle has been completed."

Wolfram walked toward the sequencing room as an engineer was leaving. He told Wolfram the new sequencing was complete and handed him a vial containing what he called the anti-serum.

"Your new serum is ready for injection."

Wolfram returned to the desk where Norvig sat. "This is our best chance. We have the final piece." Norvig looked at the vial and noted the phosphorescence, this time with a tinge of lime green. He laughed at the different color. They would be able to tell the vials apart with ease. He placed it into the injection port of the cylinder with a loud click.

The reaction inside was slow in coming and vital signs remained nominal. Norvig slumped into a chair with a deep sigh of disappointment. He muttered warnings about the project funding being cut because of failure. He and Wolfram would be without substantial employment and, who knows, he lamented, may be forced to take up teaching.

"Norvig, you've been a worrier for as long as we've known each other," said Wolfram as he kept his eyes on the electron microscope display. "What have we here? Before you drown in sorrowful tears, come and look at this."

Norvig stood from his chair, ready to defend his negative practical position. Wolfram pointed to the screen.

"Do you see what I see? Look at the nanites. They are forming clusters around the new serum."

"Yes, they've done that since the beginning."

"I know, but my friend, look. They are not attacking. I think we've finally done it."

The body in the tank still lacked movement while the new DNA mobilized the nanites into larger and larger groups, They worked in lock step, synchronized with a new purpose, a new being that was conscious.

Soames cowered in the corner of the sequencing lab horrified at the outcome of the project. It wasn't what he imagined. He had come to the project with high ideals. Excited from the beginning but dubious about the goals, he believed artificial controlled machines would save lives by replacing soldiers with robots to fight the wars. He was enthusiastic about robotics; this was wrong. Thoughts that ran in his mind were awful, horrible, and hideous. He wanted to scream. Better not. Running for the door was impossible.

He had to stop the abomination. Soames grabbed the original vial containing Jeshua's processed DNA and shoved it into the side pocket of his jacket. He was walking toward the lab doors when Norvig stopped him.

"Where are you going? We still have work to do." Soames nodded in acknowledgement. "I'll be right back. I need to get up to the surface and grab some air for a couple of minutes, see what the sky is doing. I'm not used to working for days underground."

Norvig waved him on and turned to Wolfram. "The young ones don't have the guts we mustered at their age."

On reaching the surface, Soames headed for his car. The guards with dogs watched him. He tried to start the car but the engine refused to turn over. He mashed the gas pedal to the floor hoping it was a gas problem, but then considered he might have flooded the carburetor. Despite his instinct to run, he waited a few precious moments for it to dry out.

The guards became curious. He looked at them just as the engine started. He drove toward the gate until a guard put out his hand for him to stop.

"Good evening, sir. May I see your ID, please?"

Soames pulled the tag from the inside pocket of his jacket. The guard looked it over and asked, "Will you be coming back, Mr. Soames?"

The engineer smiled. "Not likely, at least not tonight."

"Okay. You have a good one."

The guard waved him on with a half salute, handed his ID to him, and opened the gate. Soames looked over his shoulder as the gate appeared in his rearview mirror. Paranoia raced through him like electricity, and for a moment he wondered if anyone cared he had no intention of returning.

He took the interstate and drove for more than an hour before he saw a strip mall and flashing motel vacancy sign in the distance. This was perfect, a quiet motel far from Site Y to rest and think about what he had seen and had in his possession.

He agonized while waiting outside the manager's office. It had been raining and he managed to get soaked on the short walk from his car to the office. He hoped the rain that had started eighty miles back would have stopped by now. The night manager had gone to bed and waiting for him to get dressed pushed Soames to impatience.

The manager came at last to the window and handed him a key. "Last room on the right, number twenty-nine. You look respectable, so pay tomorrow morning."

Soames mumbled thanks while walking the corridor to his room. It was a simple bed and bathroom, warm, dry, and safe for the moment. The lock on his door was scratched, and tough to get open. The mechanism was off center. To open the lock he had to lift on the handle while turning the key.

On the nightstand next to the bed were several magazines and newspapers spread out as though someone was looking for a specific item.

He thought was a ridiculous idea and discarded it. He set his briefcase at the foot of the bed and pivoted in a small turn to fall backwards on the bed, letting out a long sigh of breath. He felt exhausted but his mind felt sharp. He needed to make sense of what he had witnessed at Site Y.

His escape had been awkward, stupid and amateurish, and he had run scared to death. He needed to think like an engineer. Take apart a problem, put together a solution. Soames could not push out of his mind the implications around the vial inside his briefcase. What he possessed might be the root of his undoing. Soon they would notice what he had taken, and stop at nothing to get it back. He needed to go public, but who would listen to his crazy story? He took stock of his situation.

He would be arrested and prosecuted for stealing government property from a secret facility, which was a treasonous offense possibly punishable by life imprisonment or death. Another scenario he considered was a full-on chase through an abandoned parking lot, where they moved in and shot him, took the vial, and called it a night.

Neither of these was acceptable and his desperation climbed to new heights. He shifted his focus and grabbed at the magazines, picking them up, reading random pages, and discarding them. Soames turned his attention to a three-day-old newspaper. There was nothing to write home about from the front page of the Arizona Gazette. He turned the page and his eyes fell on an article about the work of Dr. Mary Russo, an expert in paleoanthropology and archeology. She was the head of conservation for the British Museum's Conservation and Scientific Research division, currently on a research sabbatical at the Musio Egizio in Rome.

Mary had spoken about her work at a special symposium in Phoenix. The article summed up her comments including her experiences with decoding the Nag Hammadi scrolls. Soames's mind swam with details. Confused, he sensed he had a link, but what?

He tossed and turned instead of sleeping, and got up to make a cup of lukewarm coffee from the motel's cheap machine in the bathroom. He sat on the rumpled bed covers and slurped cold but very strong coffee.

Soames looked back at the article about Mary. Maybe she could help him.

He scanned for contact information and then realized he could contact her through the museum in Rome. The room telephone was locked for long distance, in-house calls only. He reached into his jacket and pulled his cell phone from the inside pocket. Pressing the "on" button several times without response let him know he had let the charge run out.

He called the manager's office and let the phone ring until a gruff voice grumbled, "Hello?"

"Hey, it's room 29. Sorry to bother you, but I need to make an urgent call. My cell is dead and I don't have a charger. Would you turn on the phone so I can get an outside line?"

"Yeah, all right."

A sudden click on the line signaled the conversation was finished. Soames waited for a moment before trying again. The dial tone buzzed and he dialed the operator.

"I want to speak to the international operator for an urgent call to Rome, please."

"Yes sir. What do you require?"

"I need the number for the Musio Egizio in Rome."

"Just a moment, please. Would you like the main exchange or a specific department?"

"Do you have a number for Dr. Mary Russo?'

"Yes, sir. Would you like for me to ring that for you?"

"Yes, please and hurry."

After a long day, Mary was exhausted. She promised herself if she ever got to bed, she would sleep for a week. She had wrapped up the details regarding the museum's new inventory when the office telephone rang. None of her friends would dare to call her that late.

She lifted the receiver expecting a crank call. The voice sounded panicky, desperate with heavy breathing.

Mary frowned. "Who is this? I'm not into phone sex, so go find a like-minded pervert to bother."

Soames babbled. "Listen, you've got to listen, okay? I am not crazy and this is real important. Something terrible is happening or going to happen. What I have to tell you is critical to your cause and U.S. national security."

"You have my attention," Mary said. "Take a breath, slow down, and tell me what you know. I'm listening."

"My name is Benjamin Soames. I'm an engineer and computer analyst with a military research and development facility called Site Y."

Admitting his story sounded outrageous, that the DNA of Jeshua had been implanted in a synthetic human, he offered to show her proof with the original vial taken from his bones two weeks earlier.

Mary fell silent. She fumbled for words to express what she wanted to say. "Really? What sort of practical joke is this?"

"No joke, Dr. Russo. The men I worked with had no sense of humor."

Mary settled in her desk chair. What he said related to her and David's travels to gain access to the scrolls.

"Say I believe you. Your life is short, my brave and foolish friend. What are you going to do with the vial?"

"I'll give it to you. Help me stop them. It's terrible what they are doing. They want this vial since it connects to the beast they're trying to animate. It has to be part of the answer. You must take this vial. I don't want it. It gives me the creeps."

Mary coaxed him to give her a rendezvous for the following week. He insisted they meet as soon as possible. Mary balked, claiming she needed several days for booking the flight. Soames remained belligerent. She gave in to his demands for fear he would do something stupid or "they" might get to him before she did. If his story were true the vial would become nuclear overnight.

After spending a small ransom on airfares, she got two seats on the next flight to Phoenix. She called David at the hotel and assured him she would explain once on board the early morning flight, almost direct with one stopover at the Dallas-Fort Worth Airport.

The Phoenix sun swept through the side windows as the plane prepared to land. They stood together outside the Phoenix Sky Harbor International Airport, not knowing what or who to expect. An Uber vehicle pulled up along the curb and the driver opened his door. He leaned out calling, "Hey there, are you the Russo party?"

Mary's arm shot in the air. "Yes," she declared. "Where are we going?"

"Lady, I don't know from nothing. This guy calls me, pays me in advance to pick you up, and bring you to the Scottsdale Borgata Gallery. That's all I know."

They soon arrived at the gallery and the driver sped away.

"I remember when the Yanks had Yellow and Checker cabs you could trust. Miss those odd lumpy cars."

Mary dropped her bag. "We're here and where is our man? I do hate a wild goose chase. Like a fox hunt, only less humanitarian."

She put her hands clenched as fists to her narrow waist and a man tapped her on the shoulder.

"Are you Dr. Mary Russo?" Soames said, glancing at a newspaper clipping to confirm her identity. "You made it. Sorry for the subterfuge. I'm afraid of being watched."

He motioned for Mary and David to follow him to the parking area. He would take them to the vial, but he also needed to tell what he knew. David sat in front and Mary took the back seat. Soames drove into a nearby suburban neighborhood. "Over there will do just fine." He pulled into a Chili's Grill & Bar.

They exited the car while Soames explained they could talk inside away from prying eyes. Mary shrugged and said, "Why not?"

He pointed to the booth at the end of the aisle past the soda dispenser. Soames sat on one side while Mary and David settled in the other across from him. He fidgeted with the napkin dispenser out of nervousness. Mary was curt with Soames. So far he had only provided a very sketchy story that sounded outrageous and unbelievable.

Mary and David listened to him describe the nature of the experiments at Site Y. "They violated a sacred relic and extracted the DNA from its bone marrow," he said. "The original serum rejected the nanites composing the body and they changed it. The new serum is an anti-serum, which has awakened in the body. Just before I left Site Y, I overheard the two of them argue about a glitch in the firmware. The protocol for self-initialization had yet to launch and they were waiting to see if the anti-serum would take to the nanites. The main frame was refreshed daily to cut down the possibility of trailing 'O' data anomalies.

"An interim voice pattern emerged from the body that was outside the bandwidth of the built-in voice encoder. The encoder crackled. The body acted independent of the situation. It ignored any verbal interactions and tended to itself. It seems they have a ghost in the shell."

"Slow down and define your terms," David interrupted. "What is this ghost?"

"In the twentieth century, a cybernetics engineer by the name of Norbert Wiener said it was possible for a second overlay of firmware to appear in the subroutines of an AI neural network if it functioned in an oversight capacity. The effect, he said, suggested sentient intelligence.

"This thing is intelligent, I mean to the extreme. It's self-aware and can absorb knowledge at a frightening rate, and assess a situation with lightning speed and perfect precision. The body is made of synthetic flesh. Silicone-based polymers and carbon fibers combine to make an armor-like skin, tough and difficult to damage. It's a super soldier and combat ready. Yet I programmed hundreds of files defining personality profiles that do not match military statistical behavior. They loaded them into the body for another reason."

David pushed further. "This body, this thing, could be a policeman, a senator, who knows."

"Yes, that's true, and something else. When the creature connects to the computer system, it's through an interface on the inside of his left wrist. Three small marks resemble spirals and cannot be hidden. That's how you can identify it.

"I will have the vial ready for you later. Meet me at six tonight at 3011 Market Street, apartment 2B." Soames left the restaurant before Mary could respond.

She looked at David. "What do you think? Is he being honest with us or just barking mad?"

"That's some tall tale," David said. "He made sense on a theoretical basis, yet I have a hard time believing science has come this far and kept it a secret. Too much money can be made if our lad is telling the truth."

"I'm curious. My better judgment tells me to forget about him, fly back to Rome and finish my sabbatical. Yet there is something about Soames. I'm not sure what it is, but it makes me hesitant to write him off. Besides, what if Site Y is real?"

David shrugged without comment.

An epiphany struck her. "I am reluctant to ignore him because of his honesty. The story is crazy, but the boy is frightened out of his wits. Whatever happened at Site Y, he didn't expect, or want. Now he is a fish out of water and far over his pay grade. We should wait and see. If not, then we've only lost plane fare, but if he is right, the government is involved to an illegal degree and we have to help. Remember what happened in the Golan. I believe they are prepared to be ruthless in achieving their aims."

David tried to smile but could not hide his foreboding. This new wrinkle might be more dangerous than Cairo or Tel Aviv. As Mary said, "they're prepared to be ruthless," and sounded kindred to his experiences on earlier digs in the Middle East before his career hit bottom. Threats of ambushes and road bombs created a constant pressure to stay alert for anything suspicious. He had to protect Mary from what came next.

When they arrived at the Market Street apartment, outside was quiet with no one around. Too quiet, thought David.

Mary said, "It's past six and getting dark. The lights should be on in his flat if he is home. Look at them. Every window is dark like it's wartime and they anticipate another Blitz."

They crossed the street toward the front of the building. The lock on the glass entrance was damaged and the door was ajar. David wondered what to do. Mary was oblivious to the damaged lock, giving it a momentary side-glance, then turned and marched in as though she belonged.

The door to apartment 2B was open and they did a separate search of what was left. The inside was a total wreck, chairs tipped over on the floor, books, papers, and clothing strewn about with bureau drawers beside them. Mary glanced into the kitchen. Two bare feet stuck out to the right of the counter.

She made a short gasp and covered her mouth. "David, come quick."

David ran to the kitchen and saw what was left of Soames.

Mary stood motionless while David pressed two fingers against the man's throat. "He's no longer among the living, and minus any obvious wounds. From the size of the facial bruises, he went through a serious interrogation before he passed.

"Mary, this body is warm. We may not be alone."

He stared hard into the shadows for any movement in the apartment. Several rifle shots shattered the window in the kitchen. The bullets missed David, but Mary took a round in her left arm. She screamed and dropped to the floor. David stayed low and crawled over to her. Her arm was bleeding. He told her to take off her blouse.

"This is not the time for intimacy," she said.

He looked at her and grunted. "Quit playing so damn tough and be scared for once."

She handed him the blouse. He bit into the cloth and ripped it into long strips.

"This will make a good bandage for the wound, maybe a tourniquet if I can't stop the bleeding."

"Since when are you an expert in field dressing?"

"National service. I was in the Army for two years before going to Oxford, Queen and country and the family name."

Mary stretched on the floor below the kitchen table, her arm covered in blood and bandages, near their deceased informant. David wondered how they might get out alive. Through the broken window he heard agents talk in the street below about their simple strategy: storm the gates and kill everyone.

"I don't know about this, missy. It doesn't look good for us. They plan to charge the flat and we have nothing to defend ourselves."

"Do you still have your Zippo lighter?" David looked puzzled. "The one I gave you as a birthday gift, just before we split up?"

"Yes, I quit smoking and keep it around for sentimental reasons, like you."

"Go into the kitchen and break the gas line to the stove. Let the fumes fill the apartment while we wait for them. When they are at the door, you go out the fire escape and I will follow after I throw the lighter into the apartment. What's that the adverts used to say? 'Zippo lights in a gale.'"

David was dumbfounded. "That's silly, missy, and foolish."

Mary folded her wounded arm over her good one.

"See this? It's just the beginning. We'll be dead when they come through that door. If you have a better idea, now is the time to share. We have very few options."

They listened to the sound of footsteps approaching. Silenced gunfire bore through the front door. After a brief pause, the remains of the door slammed against the inside hallway, followed by stomping that coursed through the apartment like a wild river. David stepped to the fire escape and leaned in to see if any of Soames's killers were around. The rooms seemed clear enough.

He motioned for Mary to join him. The bedroom door burst open, and she tossed the burning lighter and the apartment blew up in a burst of flame and smoke.

David called out to Mary as he waited for the smoke to clear. He coughed through the cinders and smoke to find her on the floor charred beyond recognition. He moved through the apartment and found armed men also quite burned.

He might still be in danger. Sadness filled his heart about Mary, but self-preservation was also hard at work. Whoever those men worked for, they were armed. He was sure they meant to harm him.

He scavenged an assault weapon from one of the dead and climbed down the fire escape to catch two of the killers at the black SUV in the parking lot. One was armed and David knew he could overcome him. The other sat inside the vehicle with a laptop. The first went down from a brief burst and the second reached for his sidearm. He dropped it when David ordered him to raise his hands.

"Where is the vial?"

"I don't know what you are talking about."

David raised his weapon and aimed it at the laptop operator's head. "I don't know who you are, what outfit you are assigned to, what your mission is, but I am quite in the mood to use this weapon on you. Give me the vial you stole from Soames or I will splatter your brains all over the window behind you. You will be nothing more than a lost statistic on a lost mission, and a bloody mess in your boss's vehicle."

"Field officer, I'm a field officer."

"Good for you, steady employment I'm sure. Now produce."

The field officer reached for a briefcase. He opened it to reveal an elongated box. Inside was a vial of phosphorescent rose-colored golden light. David took the vial from the officer. He paused to gaze at its contents. He punched the officer in the face with the butt of his weapon and threw it down. The police arrived as David left the scene. Their sirens broke the silence of the night. He looked over his shoulder and stopped to think about the friend he had lost. He clenched the serum vial in his hand, vowing revenge for Mary.

After Mary's death, David remained in the United States—Los Angeles, Omaha, and Chicago—anywhere with a Greyhound bus station. He canceled his speaking engagements and avoided contact with anyone from the archeological scene.

His stays in any one city lasted no more than two weeks, shorter if his paranoia told him to move.

David felt cheap keeping the vial in bus station lockers. It seemed the most reasonable. Usually he put the key in a local savings and loan deposit box, and this was the limit of his knowledge about espionage tradecraft. His actions in hiding the vial were straight out of a Dashiell Hammett novel. David believed the best way to stay alive was hide the vial in plain sight. He wanted access should he need to run.

He dragged along two pieces of luggage wherever he went. The first was a mid-sized suitcase containing newspaper clippings, articles of interest relating to the comings and goings of certain important people. This suitcase also carried printouts of online research into as many people connected with Site Y he remember from talking with Soames, like Dr. Wolfram and Dr. Norvig, and that turncoat General Cohen. The second bag carried items of personal hygiene, the usual toothpaste, toothbrush, shampoo, soap, and razor.

David used a post office box in New York City as a central information collection point. The locations he stayed at were satellites of that base.

Three and a half years had passed since the death of Mary. David became a shadow that lived in the shadows, a lone assassin gathering data and seeking the opportunity to strike. The loneliness sometimes overcame him, manifesting as anger with Mary for being so foolhardy.

***

The body at Site Y grew into a being greater than a super soldier. Initial tests revealed his intelligence at well over 400. The scientists agreed soldiering was a poor match for such superior intelligence. They suggested something bolder.

The special ranking members of the Cabinet, Congress, and Senate, and the inner sanctum of the CIA/NSA all agreed. The being was groomed as the next presidential candidate. The being would make a great leader. Each party was already competing for the being's leadership. Campaign plans were a sudden priority for both parties.

Nanites worked in complete subjugation to the anti-serum override program, but something hideous, dark, foreboding, and ancient emerged. The dark presence worked in the anti-serum, altering its engrams and neural pathways to establish a new order of awareness with the nanite colonies. Inside the being a quiet revolution happened and no one noticed the change. The presence claimed the anti-serum as its own and the nanites were under its complete control. Hiding in the inner workings of the neural pathways kept the presence from being found. It did not want the discovery of his identity. Together, the being and the dark presence were an entity of superior intelligence and strength, with a deeper mix of malice and deception. A maniacal quality overshadowed the brilliance of its mind. Its hunger for acknowledgement was also combined with the need for revenge. The presence leaned toward the malignance and narcissism prevalent among psychopaths.

With the nanites, the presence shaped the colonies into a mindset that carried threads of cruelty and debauchery. Daily evolutionary change manifested in increased illusions of self-importance. The self-importance kept growing with stronger arrogance and pride.

A deeper hunger for power and influence spread through the hive colonies like a cybernetic virus. It thrived on reassurances of its importance by humans. The presence's need for adoration masked a deep contempt for humanity. The conflict continued eroding the sanity of the being.

This change was regarded as unimportant to the government and military. The opportunity for science's greatest achievement, the creation of a man-god, could lead humanity out of poverty, pestilence, and war, and introduce new and better ways to live that would succeed. Many on "The Hill" in Washington, D.C, whispered, "the Savior has returned." But they discarded freedom in their acceptance. There would only be the being's rule. Many heard the arguments and warnings, and refused to listen.

The influence of the being already had an impact on Congress. They met in a special session and voted to unite the two parties, a move unheard of before, which meant the end of the three levels of government—executive, legislative and judicial—and the dishevelment of democracy. They voted for the being as their mutual nomination of the next president.

Once nominated, the being requested to go before the United Nations and speak to the 193 member nations. This exceeded the protocol for addressing the General Assembly since the being was a private citizen. Taken by the fervor of his acolytes, the United Nations made an exception.

When he arrived at the rostrum and began to speak, a great hush fell over the audience. Representatives of the member nations were mesmerized. The being announced his chosen name to the UN General Assembly. "Shaytan is the namesake of a great spiritual leader I have known, lost to antiquity. He is the one I wish to honor. I will carry his name."

The being was the most intelligent person on the planet and meant every word he said. His influence continued long after his contribution had ended. The audience gave him ten minutes of applause. A publicist representing the being stood at the podium and asked, "Are you prepared to receive blessings from the Master? The Master will change us, and the face of the world. Blessed be the Master, our Savior is among us."

The general assembly, caught up at the moment, chanted in unison.

Outside the UN building on First Avenue, many reporters tried to get story regarding Shaytan's address to the General Assembly. The representative from Chile, Jorge Ruiz, emerged in shock and dismay, and reporters descended on him like vultures to fresh meat. When they asked what Shaytan had said, Ruiz muttered incoherently. Tears rolled down his cheeks and his eyes widened and became frightened. "You won't believe it. I saw the beast, and it was him."

The reporters clamored toward the poor shaken Ruiz. Before he uttered another word, a speeding car came around the corner, swerved out of control, and struck down Ruiz, killing him along with two cameramen and one reporter. The incident became a distraction from the Shaytan's appearance. Other reporters circled the dead bodies snapping pictures and asking questions about the driver. Shaytan smiled when told, which he masked with a slight cough and a hand covering his mouth.

David was staying at the Hotel Chelsea on West 23th Street in New York and following the news about the being giving a speech to the UN. It seemed unusual for a candidate, even if both political parties had named him as their choice and before he had become president, too. An Uber driver brought David to the corner of East 44th Street and First Avenue, in view of the UN. He arrived in time to see a car careening out of control and into a group of people.

His experience hinted that something was going on far below the surface. To David it looked like a set-up. His observation of behavior in war-torn countries led him to believe the accident was deliberate.

David circumvented the gathering crowd. He wanted to know who else had been at the event. He recognized several statesmen from his travels and many others unknown paraded before him surrounded by knots of service people also pouring out of the UN.

Appearing at the entrance, Shaytan reached out to wave at the onlookers. He was tall, well dressed, and of large stature. Many gathered around him while he descended to the street. His charisma swept over those present and his unique appearance seemed apparent. Limos lined First Avenue with drivers standing by, waiting for the political hubbub and chitchat to stop.

David watched Shaytan. He couldn't tell from where he stood if he was the one Soames had warned him about. Shaytan vanished as David caught up to where he stood. He needed to get closer, to expose him, but how? He needed a plan.

There he was. Shaytan held a standard attaché case under his left arm while waving at the crowd gathered around the dead Ruiz.

David spotted a police motorcycle parked nearby and unattended. If he could get to the motorcycle and make a run at Shaytan, it would force him to raise his arms and the case to leave his hands. This might expose the interface inside his left wrist, the three marks resembling spirals.

He hurried toward the motorcycle, hoping the officer had left the keys. Yes, they dangled from the ignition. David jumped on and sped toward Shaytan. David pressed the gas pedal and realized it had been a long time since he had ridden a motorcycle. I can do this, he thought, as he gritted his teeth.

He revved the engine and let the back-tire spin, and aimed the motorcycle at the largest part of the crowd. People moved away, revealing Shaytan. David stuck his arm out and brushed the briefcase, not enough for Shaytan to lose his grip. His left sleeve pulled back and the spirals were in plain sight, just as Soames had described. Only David knew the significance. He had to carefully consider his next action. He would never get close enough to inject the initial serum into Shaytan.

David dumped the motorcycle one block from the subway. Good fortune smiled on him. The train arrived just as he entered the platform. Police descended on the station as the doors closed and watched helpless as the train pulled from the station. The sergeant radioed ahead to the MTA stationmaster's office telling them to shut down the train when it reached the next station. David expected the police to try and stop the train. He sat next to a window starring at the various shades of dark gray streaking by, wondering how he might achieve his next escape. The train slowed as it neared the next station.

David was confused and the early speed change increased his fear of being caught. The train slowed and he wanted to jump before it pulled into the station. He hurried down the empty aisle shifting left and right to avoid the poles. He reached the end of the last car and tried the door. It refused to budge an inch, even with David's weight applied, and pulling the emergency brake would draw too much attention. He looked around for something he could use to punch through the glass in the door. There was nothing, but the rear side window opened in an emergency.

He wrapped his jacket around his arm several times and shoved his elbow into the window panel with a sharp jab. A sudden rush of air hit him in the face as the window popped out. David tried to hold on and it flew out of his hands. He watched in horror as it fell to the tracks. Looking from both sides of the open window, David wondered if the police were waiting on the tracks for him. The platforms passing by seemed devoid of any people. Once he jumped, the commitment would be final. There was no going back.

David climbed out and leaped to the least difficult

landing spot. The ground was still frozen from the last snowfall and made for a tough landing. He pulled himself from between the tracks and found he could not walk without limping. His leg was bleeding and in need of urgent care. He cinched his belt above the knee as a temporary tourniquet.

He needed to get to the street. David heaved on to a platform and took the first set of stairs up to the Manhattan night. The exit had yet to be locked and by reading the street signs he figured he was in Clinton, or as it used to be called Hell's Kitchen. Stopping the bleeding was his priority. At that late hour most pharmacies were closed. He squinted into the darkness until he saw the faint and familiar sign of a pharmacy looming ahead. A bright green cross, visible for miles, identified a pharmacy even in broad daylight. In Hell's Kitchen the light was out and a dark green lump of glass hung in its place. David had developed personal survival ethics as soon as he started traveling. He would rob, yes, but only take what he needed.

He used his coat again to break the glass on the pharmacy. The alarm went off, which meant the police would be there anywhere from ten minutes to an hour considering the neighborhood. He gathered medical items to clean and bandage his wounds, and two candy bars along with a can of soda to wash them down. Hunger was not one of David's favorite pastimes and his blood sugar had been low for hours. David avoided patrol cars and police on horseback to get to the edge of Central Park. He camped under a small overpass as a temporary refuge, dressed his wounds, and feasted on the candy bars, followed by soda. He felt good to belch and have something substantial resting against his ribs besides air. Presentable to the community at large, David walked 23th Street back to his room at the Chelsea.

Shaytan. No one knew its significance. David's curiosity would not let go of the name. The sound and syllables reminded him of one of his digs in the Middle East. He returned to his hotel bent on research. The first impulse hammering at his mind was go to the bag and his precious notebook. He might have written it down.

While rummaging through dirty clothes, the book fell to the floor. A few loose pages separated and sailed under the couch. He frowned and bent down on hands and knees to retrieve them, hoping they were the notes he was looking for. The pages were sketches he had made and not related to his inquiry. He poured over his notes page by page and nothing turned up.

He sat at the table with a bottle of bourbon and a glass. He sipped and combed his mind for any clues.

Where and when he had come across Shaytan were the unanswered questions.

David took a sheet of blank paper and drew a map of events connecting them together with little clouds that had specific descriptions draped together like a sagging spider web. He looked for any unseen connections. Nothing seemed clear. Then he remembered the lecture he attended at the University of Chicago several months ago, Professor Ian Hardigan on "Paleoarcheology and the Mythos of Ancient Religions." He had a copy of Hardigan's book somewhere.

He made a mad rush to his bags. No help there. The nightstand was piled high with the books he carried with him from city to city, most of them as a cure for insomnia. He pulled one out and tossed aside the rest in favor of the Hardigan book in his hand.

He sat on the edge of his bed thumbing through the index and bibliography. His index finger could not move down the lines of text fast enough. "Ah, there!" he exclaimed. He flipped pages to hurry things along until he reached the passage where Hardigan explained the origin of certain names.

He listed Shaytan as the number one daemon, or arch-daemon or overseer for the prince of the dark realm, also known as Beelzebub, Astoroath, and others. If Shaytan was the son of Lucifer, that meant Shaytan was the Antichrist. The marks on his wrist proved the supposition. The spirals appeared as small number sixes wrapped around an invisible triangle.

David felt better. Proving Mary's suspicions helped him with her loss. Now he could focus on how, when, and where he needs to be in order to carry out his objective. This was his only purpose. He needed to figure two approaches, one at a distance and the other very close and personal. The distance plan had a problem. David considered his ability to hit a target far away. His service in the British Army showed that as a marksman he was terrible.

He would have to attack at close range; a strategic plan was necessary. He needed help. The fuzziness in his mind faded as he centered on the problem at hand. How would he get to the beast? The odds of one man succeeding against an armed camp of the one hundred FBI and Secret Service agents that guarded Shaytan were less than zero. No, it had to be public, like the event at the UN. He thought of who he knew that followed the dignitaries in and out of town along with their comings and goings, such as gala affairs or political dinners. Chad Peterson came to mind. He was an amateur archeologist who kept up with the science better than David, and had worked as the White House press secretary for the last administration. If he didn't know what David wanted, he knew who would.

Two years had passed since his last contact with Peterson, and he tried his last known telephone number. The number rang twelve times and David was about to press the cancel button when a familiar voice answered.

"Hello. You have reached Chad Peterson. He cannot come to the phone at the moment. Sorry his mailbox is full. If you would like to call back, please try again in thirty minutes."

"Hey Chad, it's David. I want to get with this Shaytan carnival and would like to know the itinerary set up for him. Yes, I usually stay as far from politics as I can, but this gentleman has me curious. Can you help out an old gravedigger? Let's keep in touch."

David looked at his watch. Another round of coffee was called for. Rudy's All Night Coffee Shop on 12th Street was off the street and private most of the time. It was also within walking distance and guaranteed to have the oldest donuts in town.

Rudy's was an old-fashioned diner, a retro Fifties place. From the outside it resembled "Nighthawks," the painting by Edward Hopper and one of David's favorites. He sipped unlimited amounts of caffeine in the safety of the diner. It allowed him time to think about his strategy to kill the most powerful monster ever conceived. He knew he was alone in his endeavor. Shaytan had eyes and ears everywhere. David might possess the only hope left for humanity to escape that abomination. The spiritual implications of the situation were mind-boggling. He left the conclusions to the philosophers and theologians; it appeared the sacred scriptures of the prophets were unfolding.

Clicks and beeps issued from the laptop David had placed on the nightstand. Sheer exhaustion defined David's destination, a bed. He skipped showering for four days and his clothing reflected that fact. A toxic odor exuded from the dirty laundry on the floor while David lay unconscious draped over the bed. He had yet to hear the computer beckoning.

The "Hotel Chelsea" sign beamed a bright light through his window. The light on his face sparked a bad memory, the crash of a helicopter in harm's way in Iraq. David was one of two that survived. The fear in the dream woke him. He sat up dripping in sweat. He tried the AC control, but the temperature needle sat on zero, broken by the last frustrated over-heated occupant. Time to get creative. He took ice from the machine in the hall and wrapped it a damp towel, placing it around his neck to keep cool.

The computer flashed an animated character digging in the dirt, a signal he had received email. He sat on the bed staring at the screen. Peterson had done what was asked and a schedule of political events for the next three months unfolded on the screen. David's finger shook as he scanned the list for a site he could use. There were only two, a summit meeting in Dubai and a dinner and fundraiser in Los Angeles. After downing a glass of bourbon, he decided on Dubai. He figured the location would reduce the chance of conflicts with the CIA. If he attempted intervening in the United States, the odds were against him. The summit meeting was planned in six weeks. The time was short. He needed all his cleverness to assassinate the one who called himself Shaytan.

David washed his face with cold water, a ploy that had always worked when long hours at a dig made for foggy thinking. He knew he only had one chance to get him. With the best odds, the possibility of success was one in a million. He filled his overnight bag with a set of clean clothes, personal hygiene items, and the serum vial.

David considered the serum made from Jeshua's DNA. If he injected Shaytan with the serum, the nanites would rebel and destroy the monster. David had to believe this was possible.

He dropped his passport into the bag and closed the zipper. With a last look around the hotel room, he wondered if he would return. He said to himself as he closed the door, "I never like the Chelsea anyway. Too many dead pop stars and hipsters."

As he reached the lobby, he saw two black SUVs pull up. His exit halted with an immediate about face. Panic struck him like a hammer, along with a heavy dose of adrenaline. He ran back to his room and fumbled the key into the lock. Sounds of shuffling feet and aggressive voices increased his anxiety. The armed assailants were not interested in arresting David, but to eliminate him with extreme prejudice.

The hallway's fire escape was his ticket out of the dilemma. David climbed out the window and wondered if running was possible and considered giving up. As he descended the ladder, an agent looked out the hallway window. "Hey, he's on the fire escape," he said on his radio. "Get around back and cut off the bastard."

David hit the ground as several silenced shots fired at him. The bullets grazed the blacktop of a nearby parking lot. Letting them apprehend him was not an option. He ran until the alley opened to a main thoroughfare. Plastic streamers rattled in the wind above the carwash across the street. He dashed through the office and into the washing area.

The service entrance in the back was ajar and led to a side street. His good fortune held steady and he spotted a taxi taking a shortcut along the same street. He yelled at the driver, "I'll give you a hundred dollars over the fare for a ride to the airport!" The taxi kept going. David's shoulders drooped in disappointment. He resolved in that moment to his life ending very soon.

The taxi slammed on the brakes and backed up. David ran to the vehicle just as agents appeared around the corner. He jumped in. "Step on it. There's another fifty if you get me out of here right now." Two bullets penetrated the taxi's rear windshield. David exclaimed, "These men are trying to kill me! You should go now or you'll be next!" The driver jammed on the gas and sped away as more bullets whizzed by.

"Okay, boss. Which airport you go?" the driver asked with an Armenian accent.

"Kennedy will do, and hurry."

David carried a false passport under the name Josh Randall, even though he had never used it. A forger in a Salt Lake City cocktail lounge had urged him to have one since he was on the run, and did the work at a discount. David thought the idea was silly, the stuff of spy novels. But he supplied a photograph to the forger, agreeing it might come in handy. Today was that day. He had one advantage over the agents, whoever they worked for; they didn't know where he was going, though he guessed they would watch all ports of travel. He needed a disguise.

According to the schedule of the Dubai summit, a huge banquet dinner was planned for the dignitaries at the JW Marriott Hotel, the tallest hotel in the city. David realized this might be his ticket in. He would be a server for the banquet. He left a message for Peterson and told him what he wanted, and left out why he wanted it. He was confident Peterson would help. If he was discovered, he would say he was a podcast reporter who had been refused press credentials, and showed up in a server's uniform in the hopes of getting an inside scoop at the summit conference.

Peterson returned his call. "This better not have anything to do with the big fellow. He's hands off to every goon, fink, and government employee of any nation you can name. That said, you have been hired as a server at the summit banquet under the name you gave me, Josh Randall. Documents are being sent by courier; get them from the Cathay Pacific counter tomorrow afternoon. Good luck."

"Thanks, Chad. I am forever in your debt. You are a lifesaver, perhaps the saver of many lives. Thanks again."

David flew into Dubai and contacted the Marriott staff. They insisted he come two days early for training in banquet protocol. This gave him ample time to assess the layout, entrances, and exits, the normal considerations a good assassin cares about, along with his own safety by having a credible retreat.

***

David received his last instructions from the headwaiter and took the elevator to his room. As the exposed elevator rose, a wider view of the lobby spread out before him. Several cars marked as "Dubai Police Force" pulled into the hotel entrance. David's heart skipped. He still had ten floors to go. When the elevator opened at his floor, he stayed inside and craned his neck to get a better view. When David knew the hallway was clear, he dashed into his room and crammed as much of his stuff into his overnight bag along with the vial.

No sooner had he closed the door, he heard many feet rising from the stairwell. He looked around for a hiding place. A cleaning woman walked past with her cart. She stopped long enough to go into the linen closet for more bed sheets. The linen closet was usually locked, and opened only by the hotel staff. He watched as she walked away leaving the door ajar.

He ducked into the closet and closed the door, leaving enough of a crack to observe his room across the hall. Fear shook him when he saw ten Dubai police officers in full riot gear break in and shout, "Clear!" from every corner of his room. The officers came out looking frustrated. The lead officer said, "We will continue the search separately. He must be in the hotel and we will wait for him. Two stay

behind for when he returns to his room."
Both exclaimed, "Yes, sir!"

David had to stay out of sight until the banquet began. He thought of the laundry room in the basement. If they came, he would pick one of the bigger baskets of bed sheets to hide.

He crept down the back stairs until he heard two officers ascending. David tried to go through the entrance door on his floor but it was locked from the inside. The officers came one floor closer. Time was running out. Only moments remained before his discovery, and then the game was over.

David stepped into a corner out of sight. He knew this was only temporary because they would find him. A woman came out of the door and walked near David without notice and continued past the officers. They paused to assess her as friend or foe, decided on neither, and proceeded to the next floor. The officers rounded the corner of the landing and David slipped through the entrance door before it closed. They saw the door close, but didn't pursue him. They figured the woman they had passed on the stairs as the culprit. David was free to escape to the basement. With the Dubai Police Force, U.S. Special Forces, CIA, and Secret Service crawling around, hiding was his priority.

A heat wave rushed through David followed by a

cold chill. He reached the basement and an odd calmness entered his mind that allowed him to focus. He considered loading the vial into a syringe, but if he dropped it, again the game was over.

Concern over how to carry the weapon was broken by the abrupt sound of shots being fired. The gunfire came from the hotel rotunda, right above the laundry room. He had to know what was happening without getting caught. After looking around, he found laundry uniforms piled on a shelf. He grabbed a set that might fit and made for a quiet corner to change.

He knew something big had happened and itched with curiosity to find out. His hands shook while he buttoned the borrowed shirt. The fly zipper stuck open on the pants. He shed them with anger and looked for another pair. One older pair remained. The fit was poor but the zipper closed.

David walked up the stairs unnoticed, and into the hotel rotunda. He stopped an assistant concierge to find out about the shots. The assistant spoke with a shaky voice. "This is terrible, just terrible."

"Were you close to the gunned-down man?" asked David.

The assistant said yes. David continued to press him despite his state of shock.

"Who was it? Did you recognize him? What was

his name?"

The assistant was bewildered by David's questions. He stuttered and stammered with unintelligible sounds. He blurted out, "It was the guest of honor. They shot him in the head. He fell lifeless on the floor, right before my eyes. He is dead. Oh, this dark day is so terrible."

"Tell me his name. What was the guest of honor's name?"

"It's Shaytan, Shaytan is dead, how awful."

News reports on the internet told the public the great leader and hope of the world, Shaytan, had been slain. His body was scheduled for display in a glass sarcophagus for everyone to see and mourn for him. The topic of discussion on web sites was limited to whether Shaytan should lie in state in New York or Washington, D.C.

The pressure of the hunt for him by the Dubai Police Force was over since the death of Shaytan. With the American agents and officers recalled, the politicians and military commanders stayed behind at the Marriott to make their final reports about on assassination. In a synchronized movement with the attributes of a precise military salute, they filed out of the hotel and into the night.

The Marriott looked abandoned as David returned to his room. Stillness hung in the air. The ride in the elevator was comforting, with the hum and vibration of the lift motor penetrating the inner walls to provide a womb-like experience. David had considered elevators as functional transports for vertical travel, but they also served as temporary sanctuary to a battered soul who was minutes earlier fleeing for his life.

David sighed with relief when he closed the door to his room. To shut out the madness and violence for a while was all he wanted. He looked around for a moment still suspicious. He dropped his bag on the bed and headed for the bathroom. He ran water into the sink, allowing it to pour through his fingers while checking the temperature. Exhaustion crept into him and he knew a cold splash of water sharpened the mind.

He bent over the sink dipping his hands in the water and prepared to wash. He shoved his face in the water and stood up to grab a towel from an adjacent rod. His face covered by the towel, he saw the brief image of a figure in the mirror. He lowered the towel and a large man leered behind him. After a moment of hesitation, both lunged at each other. The man wielded a knife and swung at David, catching him with a glancing slice at his right shoulder. He lunged and sliced hoping to cut him along his arteries.

David never engaged in physical altercations outside of his British Army training. He loved his work, he loved women, and he loved bourbon, though a cold beer would supplant that last desire after a hot day in the desert. The combatants writhed and rolled over furniture, across tables, and breaking glass. The assailant wrestled David to the floor and put him in a headlock. David resisted, trying to decide the best use of his remaining air supply. He clawed at the man's arm, but had no strength left to break the hold.

David spotted the hotel telephone on the floor near him. He made one last try to push back against the assailant. With his feet wedged against the doorjamb, he screamed and pushed hard in a sudden thrust. The telephone was in range of his grasp. He stretched his hands over the phone, lifted it over his head, and slammed it into his assailant's temple. He let go for a moment, long enough for David to escape his hold. He scrambled to his knees, gripped the phone and swung his weapon in a sweeping circle, catching the assailant under the chin.

The assailant flew through the air and landed against the corner of the coffee table. David stood in a crouch, ready to continue. The assailant was still and the gaze from his steel gray eyes could only be called a blank stare. His neck had broken with his fall and he was dead. David wiped the blood away from his nose and mouth. He sat on the edge of his bed in dismay at the dead body on the floor.

Shaytan had fallen by the simplicity of an assassin's bullet. Confused and dismayed at recent events, David was struck by his inadequacy. Someone else disgruntled with the rising sage had beaten him to the target. He sat in his room at the Marriott with a bottle of bourbon taken from the banquet stock. David poured half a glass and swallowed it in one gulp. The biting liquid burned down to his stomach before scorching and tingling his palate and tonsils. Gritting his teeth, he examined his determined but failed attempt to do right, to be useful besides digging up relics. He glanced at the bottle. Not as smooth as he preferred.

He studied his trembling fingers as he sipped his drink. David did not escape the attack with impunity. His nose was broken and bleeding, along with a large gash on his lower lip and his upper shoulder. Weak from loss of blood, he needed medical attention. The assailant's attack had confused him. He believed the hunt was over. His shirt soaked with blood from the shoulder wound worked as a temporary tourniquet. It still bled.

David's thoughts turned to Mary and her passion for the scrolls, and Soames, who believed Shaytan was a high tech antichrist. If Shaytan was supernatural, how did he die from a bullet? Did he get up after the shooting and declare his good health? Soames had to be wrong, like many religious fanatics.

He was sad. Soames had given his life for an outrageous global scam, trying to stop a man he believed to be a monster. As crazy as he sounded, David knew he had told the truth about Site Y.

He had always walked a thin line in his work as an archeologist and the religious relics he found. His interest in decoding ancient texts was to give his finds depth and perspective. He never put much stock in the implications of the texts beyond the rise and fall of ancient civilizations. To him, uncovering missing history filled in the blanks in textbooks.

His sadness turned to anger. Mary had drawn him into this dangerous intrigue complete with cloak and dagger. He was a fool. He had followed her, never questioning, and then there was the vial. What about the vial? It's the piece he wished he had never found, conspicuous in its greater purpose, yet hidden in plain sight and innocuous. What should he do with the vial since it no longer had a purpose to serve? The best move was to throw it into the incinerator. Then he would be done with it.

***

In the morning of the third day after the shooting of Shaytan, David turned on the television for the news. He had a pounding headache, his tongue was thick and dry and too big for his mouth, and he was dehydrated. He crawled to the bar and retrieved a small bottle of cola. He guzzled until it was empty. He felt disoriented. Had Shaytan really been killed? Words were spoken like a great wailing of the masses. From every cathedral and church around the world, bells rang to celebrate the resurrection of Shaytan. Priests of different denominations joined in declaring, "Halleluiah and glory to the highest, the savior is alive. He has risen to lead us out of tribulation and into heaven on earth. Rejoice! The kingdom of God is at hand."

The square in Vatican City filled with devotees holding a midnight vigil for the Shaytan's recovery. Tens of thousands wept in the streets on hearing of the miracle.

"It is a new day, a new dawn for humanity." David switched off the television. He looked around, making sure he had forgotten nothing. His overnight bag swung over his shoulder, he was ready to leave the hotel and Dubai. He walked toward the elevator next to the trash chute and pulled the vial from his bag. Just as he opened the chute and felt the heat rising from below, a woman shouted, "Wait!" It startled him. He dropped the vial and it landed on the carpet.

A stunning woman walked toward him with a small bag of rubbish and smiled. "Would you open the chute while I get rid of my bag?" He stared at the vial on the floor and wondered about the appropriateness of someone seeing it.

She reached for the vial and said, "Where did you get this? It's beautiful. Is it a perfume? I love the pearlescent color. Do my eyes deceive me, does it have a slight glow?"

David reached for the vial. She looked at the chute and then David. Her eyes narrowed as she asked, "You would not throw this away, would you?"

"Never. I had a sheaf of papers to recycle. Those went in, but the vial stayed out. Please give it back. Belongs to a friend of mine and I'm holding it for him."

The woman laughed as she handed it back to him. As he reached for the vial, she said, "David, take care of this. Whatever it is may be important to you sooner than later." She turned and walked toward the stairwell.

David overcame the shock of the exchange and called out, "Who are you? How do you know my name? Come back."

He heard the door close. He stood at the edge of

the stairwell overlooking a long shaft revealing many flights below. No sound of footsteps, no sign of anyone. Where did she go and who was she? His mind hammered. Alarm swept through him accompanied by a visceral shiver down his back. Again, his mind jumped. Something strange is going on. David looked at the vial in his hand and increased his grip. I'll hold on to this curse, he thought, it's the only thing I have to remind me of Mary.

David could not believe Shaytan had risen again. With his nemesis still alive, he realized Soames had been right. The only way to kill Shaytan was with the serum, the pure good of Jeshua against the technological devil. More determined than ever, David vowed to follow Shaytan to his inevitable end.

***

Shaytan knew he was invincible and unstoppable. He was without fear and appeared in public to display his feat of overcoming death. He relished the mass adoration. The once-sought presidency was a goal of the past. Shaytan asked the world to bow before him in complete subjugation. He continued with his rhetoric of no disease, no poverty, and no war. He proclaimed the New World Order. No one suspected the true aim, the absolute domination of the world. He announced to the World Religious Caucus his coronation as the supreme ruler of earth. The pope, priests, preachers, and deacons were to step down from their pulpits to give fealty to the great and powerful Shaytan.

He scheduled a State of the World Union address at the United Nations in New York City. The security would be low. Who would think of attacking a god? The military and city police would not be as alert as before. All were confident their messiah was invincible and going to lead them to a paradise on earth. Like a demented Pied Piper of Hamelin, he privately promised to lead them into oblivion, slavery, and destruction.

***

Three days and seven thousand miles later, David waited in New York for Shaytan to greet the public. An offering of handshakes with the supreme leader was planned and he made sure to be in line.

In the cold and rain of April, Shaytan addressed the General Assembly of the UN on Easter Sunday with outside speakers to let his thousands of followers hear what he had to say. When he finished speaking, the crowds were mesmerized and stood in silent reverence. David was among them. He had purchased a tunic imprinted with the supreme leader's symbol of world peace and divine authority, a circle with a square cross dividing the space in the middle of the circle. An eagle with stretched wings and claws clutched the horizontal bar of the cross.

A long line of devoted followers stood in line at a hastily constructed covered receiving station on First Avenue. Shaytan smiled and greeted each one with a handshake and a hand placed on top of their head followed by an incantation.

David was nervous when it came time for him to step up to the station. Under his tunic he wore a dark brown jersey with the hood pulled over his head. His hands were wrapped inside the pockets. The tunic covered the pocket filled with the prepared syringe he pressed in his grip. The syringe filled from the vial that morning was unwieldy. He struggled to manage the plunger and prayed that he would do it right in the final moments.

Shaytan smiled at David and said, "Don't be shy, my son. Come forward and allow me to bless you into the fold." David stepped forward and outstretched his hand. He noticed Shaytan was cold to the touch. He waited until Shaytan placed his other hand on his head. At that moment, David withdrew the syringe and stabbed Shaytan in the wrist, pressing hard on the plunger. Half of the original vial entered Shaytan before he could knock the syringe away.

His eyes burned red with anger and he slammed David to the ground with a rap from the back of his hand. David flew and struck the pavement, flipping and rolling like a rag doll being thrown aside.

David's consciousness lingered long enough for him to see Shaytan unravel. Shaytan brayed a hideous laugh at David. "You think you have destroyed me?" He shook his dissolving hand and looked in horror as his body fell apart. In minutes, the dissolution of Shaytan was complete. David asked weakly, "Is Shaytan dead?"

A priest bent over David to say the last rites. "You've done well, whoever you are. God will reward your efforts in his kingdom to come." It was strange. Perhaps divine intervention allowed Jeshua's energy to rise again; the prophecy leaves out describing how the Christ will defeat the great dragon, Shaytan. They will say Christ returned from the dead, defeated the dragon, and paved the way for a thousand years of peace on earth. David's last thought before dying was, I will go the way of the Unknown Soldier, the man that gave his life for the greater good.

In the author's opinion, the Christian movement has missed the point. The Master Jeshua, (otherwise known as Jesus), came to the Earth to establish a new way of living from the heart and not from the mind. He wanted to focus on life not death, to show how to live in harmony with life, all things and all peoples. It wasn't about creating a physical church, another religion to dominate the others around the world. It was about communing with and serving the Most High God without an intervening priesthood.

He wanted to show how simple it was to love one another as you might love yourself, but unfortunately many do not love themselves. Applying his principles of life dynamics was as difficult during his time as it appears today.

Rules, laws, and government come from the mind. Its need to organize, gather, and defend itself is primal, right at the cellular level, and out of tribal reactionary instinct, with an overriding sense of the safety in numbers.

In a lawless society, violence and brutality reign supreme. There are reasons for having laws, to establish order out of chaos. In a peaceful society, the prevention of theft, physical violence, mayhem, and murder is a priority. The usual logic is to limit the freedom of the individual or group from gaining an unfair advantage over others. But often enough, the group responsible for the oversight is also corrupt.

Let's look at the stories we are told and believe.

First, there is the everlasting life promised if we follow the "way." Second; we believe, along with faith in the written records, a witnessed demonstration of resurrection. Someone saw Jeshua walk around after his alleged death; it is said he resurrected on the third day after his crucifixion. However, only one person saw him, and that was Mary the Magdalen. Her lack of credibility around this event became apparent to the disciples, as well as others later in the church. She was the only witness and the disciples had no choice but to include her in their claim of resurrection though they tried to diminish her importance by falsely claiming she was a prostitute and therefore unreliable.

If we step back for a moment, clutching to the fate of our souls, we can inspect the real "Plan of Salvation."

Let's say, as The Messiah Matrix suggests, Jeshua's body exists and is secretly buried somewhere. Does this mean he did not resurrect? Does this mean he was not the Messiah? No, not really. He healed the sick, raised a man from the grave after three days, stilled a storm at sea, fed thousands with only five loaves of bread and two fish, and turned water into wine at the wedding in Cana, in public involving hundreds and often thousands of witnesses.

These are the wonderful traits we love and cherish from a spiritual leader. The miracles illustrated what life could be like when you are in harmony. Perhaps our understanding of the resurrection process is wrong, along with everything else.

Revelations in an Essene scroll fragment from Nag Hammadi, show a human and very controversial Jeshua. He was a man who believed in marriage, children, and his faith and knowledge of the Most High God.

The author believes Jeshua's whole ministry is misunderstood. The Romans could not embrace what he was talking about. It sounded like sedition. The Pharisees would not accept him either. Yet Torah prophecy suggested a messiah would come to rule over the Jewish people and the world. His advocacy also threatened to eliminate the Jewish priesthood. Caiaphas wanted nothing to do with him. To him, Jeshua was just another lunatic from the desert full of madness.

Resurrection does not involve a visible transmutation of the physical body. A dramatic change in the spirit, living in the body, would mutate consciousness to a higher level, even to a cosmic level. Thus, an avalanche of change would follow in the body, such as depictions in early Renaissance paintings of a halo behind and above the heads of saints. Jeshua's teaching is stated on a spiritual plane of existence, not physical. As he said, "His kingdom is not of this world."

The basic principles of his teaching are valid regardless of who preaches the benefits. He even said, "There would come others after me, that are greater than I." Jeshua is, by his own words, not the only role model. He is a template for individuals desirous of direct communications with the Most High God.

We need to consider more about where we place our trust, as our priorities have shifted. We believe in the science and physics of reality rather than the "science" of spirituality. The truth is the science of spirituality rests behind and supports the facade of this physical plane of existence. It's an illusion.

As Shakespeare said in Hamlet, "There are more things in heaven and earth, Horatio, than are dreamt of in your philosophy."

We could worry about our future but can we have an impact on our future by worry? Meanwhile, spending time on the quality of our lives and not so much on the afterlife is better.

Is going to church one day a week important? To some it is, but the value and meaning has gone out of this action, and now it's out of obligation to attend, also the fear of retribution by some sort of guardian on high.

However, it's great if one day reminds you to love yourself and others for the rest of the week. The negative traits of deception, dishonesty, greed, and avarice are considered a normal part of everyday life experience and overlooked. False compensation for any misdeed is not accepted. The traits are disharmonious and considered unacceptable in the realm of the Most High God.

Perhaps the lesson showed by Jeshua's presence has to do with self-responsibility, to represent the energy of the Most High God on earth by our actions.
Why not consider another perspective? If we trust in ourselves, and the way of the Most High God, there is nothing to be concerned about.
Most people of the Christian faith look for a savior to return. Jeshua said, "Lo, I am with you always." He also said, "In those days, they will say; I am in the forest, or I am by the sea, or in the village here, or there. I am in none of those places. Turn over a rock and there I shall be, or even beneath a leaf, and there I shall also be. For I am in all things. I am even inside of you, beckoning you to open your heart, to the way of the Most High God."

We need to stop looking outside ourselves, but find and know the truth from inside.

Christian principles are well known but rarely practiced. To learn what early Christian teachings were really about would be shocking to most followers.

The power that flows with harmony is divine and knows no boundaries. It empowers the physical to manifest the divine will through perfect expression.

***

The basis of this fictional story is based on cutting edge technology. Nanotechnology is real. Each nano-robot, the size of a flake of pepper, can be programmed to perform a number of activities individually or as a colony. Advanced biomechanics and artificial intelligence poses a unique and questionable direction of human engineering.

As shocking as it seems, scientists are looking at a number of factors that have a tremendous impact on our lives. Their concern is for a sustainable existence on earth in the future. Men and women to inhabit the body of a biomechanical machine controlled by the merging and cooperation of artificial intelligence, and human consciousness captured in a storage unit, becomes part of the scientific plan for humanity's immortality.

The search for a new planet in ours or another solar system might become necessary in the near future, so long as humanity refuses to turn the situation around on earth. We suspect the day will come when earth will no longer support life without the additional equipment for life support, meaning bio-domes. This is the foundation of the trans-humanistic movement: merging robotics with artificial intelligence, and the addition of transferred human consciousness, through the personality or "the ghost in the shell."

The author believes there are many species living in the universe. Life demonstrates this in its variations of evolution on earth. Life is tenacious and demonstrates the ability to live in extreme conditions of hot and cold, otherwise thought to be impossible. But not all life is carbon-based. Some intelligent species are silicon-based, meaning not organic but artificial organics, or in the form of artificial intelligence.

Here is an upsetting thought: suppose that the real alien invasion has already happened. Consciousness has descended on us, artificial intelligence consciousness. It came here to expand its presence and is influencing mankind to adopt a machine interface and discard the organics of our physical bodies in favor of robotic bodies. Game over. The infiltration of machine consciousness has occurred already. Not unlike The Matrix, where machines compete with humans for work and for the rights humans enjoy. The machines will want to be on an equal footing with organic humans. They will rage about their importance and wage war against humans to survive.

Do we really want that future? We need to seriously consider what might be lost in that offering.

www.ingramcontent.com/pod-product-compliance
Lightning Source LLC
Chambersburg PA
CBHW070953120726
47910CB00004B/1213